Little Red and the Lumpy Bed

Dreaming Princesses, Book 3

Books by C. Rae D'Arc

Dreaming Princesses

Dreaming Beauty
Fairest and the Frog
Little Red and the Lumpy Bed

* * *

Haunted Romance

Don't Date the Haunted
Don't Marry the Cursed
Don't Dance with Death
"Oz's Haunting Survival Book"

Royal Families of Rezhina Valley

King Rezhnum & Queen Venizhus Reo of Somnus

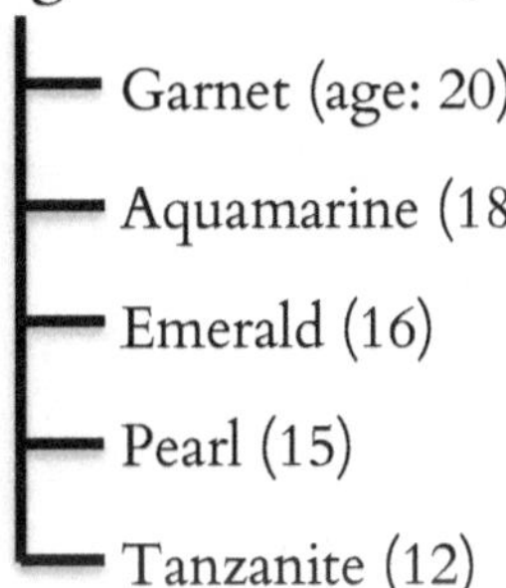

- Garnet (age: 20)
- Aquamarine (18)
- Emerald (16)
- Pearl (15)
- Tanzanite (12)

King Eric & Queen Candice Fashio of Ormio

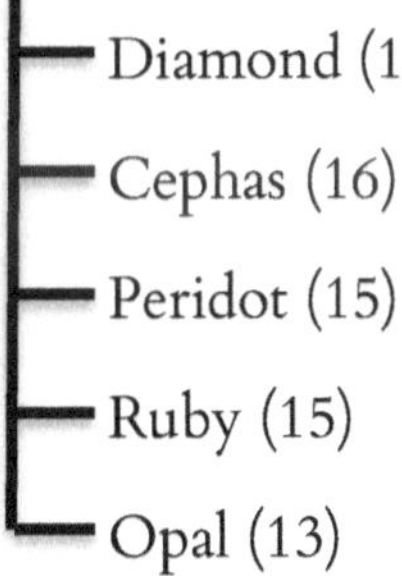

- Diamond (18)
- Cephas (16)
- Peridot (15)
- Ruby (15)
- Opal (13)

King Leroy & Queen Rhiannon Zhenero of Huiess

- Amethyst (19)
- Sapphire (14)
- Topaz (13)

LITTLE RED
AND THE
LUMPY BED

DREAMING PRINCESSES, BOOK 3

C. RAE D'ARC

To my ASL professors and student aides.
Thanks for opening my eyes to the Deaf culture.

Map of Somnus

and surrounding kingdoms

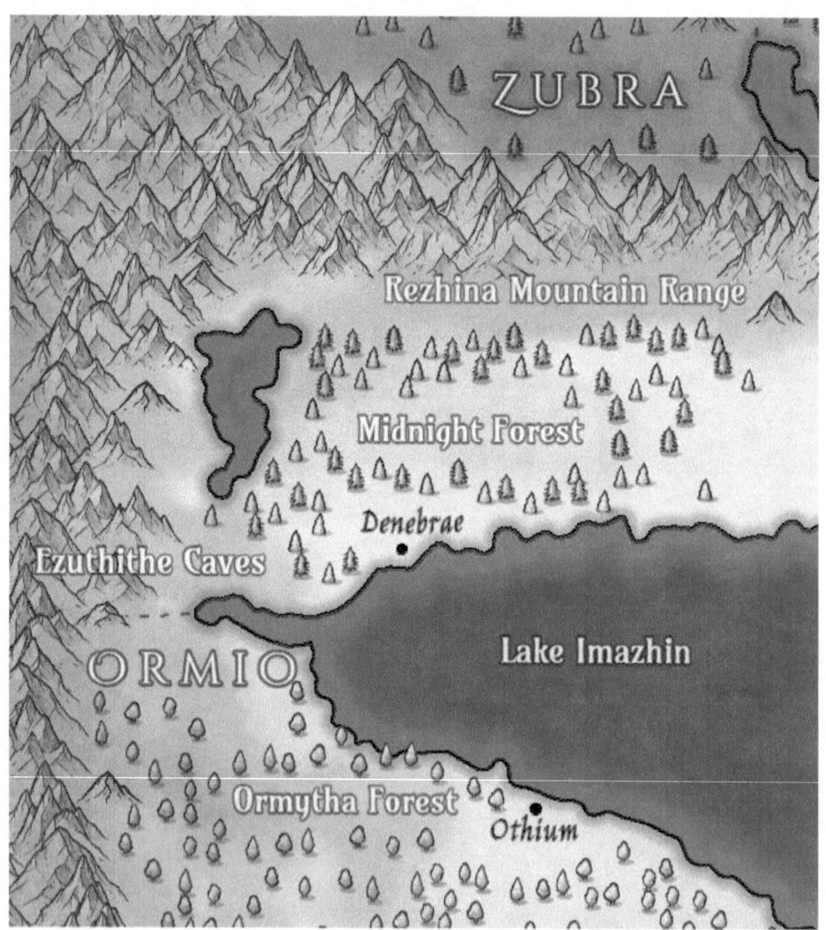

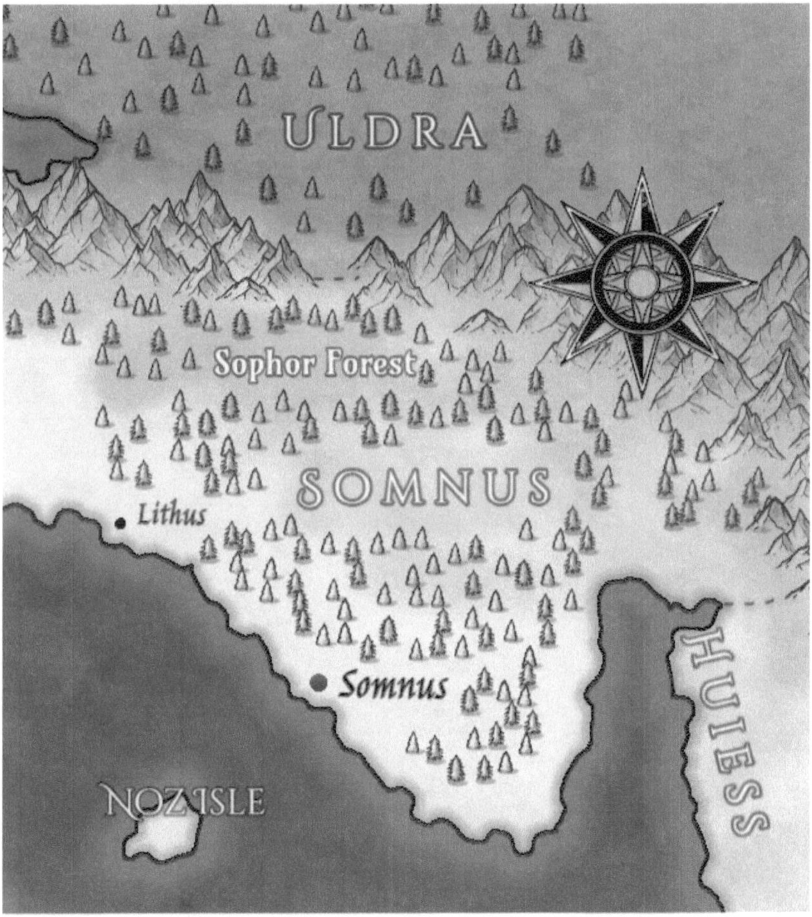

ULDRA
Sophor Forest
SOMNUS
Lithus
Somnus
NOZISLE
HUIESS

Little Red and the Lumpy Bed

Dreaming Princesses, Book 3

C. Rae D'Arc

PART 1

"Then she took, first, twenty mattresses,
and laid them one upon the other on the three peas, and
then she took twenty feather-beds more, and put these
again a-top of the mattresses. This was the bed the
Princess was to sleep in."

- *The Princess and the Peas*, by Hans Christian Anderson

Chapter 1

DOT

Who knew a simple pea under a pile of mattresses could be so irritating? I did. I had always been extra sensitive to clothing seams, loud sounds, and even subtle facial cues. While these observations helped me empathize with others, they also made it annoyingly difficult to get a full night's sleep. I often tossed and turned in my bed for hours, wishing to sleep peacefully.

Unlike Emer. I was actually jealous of her long rest. I remembered the day she was poisoned all too well.

"Canceled?" my dad, the King Eric Fashio of Ormio, boomed. He wasn't a terribly tall man (maybe one and three-quarters of a meter in the morning), but he had the powerful voice of a king. I winced as his outburst echoed through the welcome chamber of Somnus castle, partly from the sound and partly from the hint of anger in his voice. "You are canceling the entire night of festivities to celebrate your own daughter's birthday after we—her honored guests—traveled all this way?"

No one else in my family of seven seemed overly stimulated by Dad's outburst or our surroundings. The stony room seemed cold despite the many wall torches (one flickered with dying flames), thick rugs of jeweled designs beneath our dance shoes (was there a pattern, and how often did it repeat itself?), and draping green curtains framing the stained-glass windows (did they depict any birds in the art?).

Perhaps the chilly sensation came from King and Queen Reo's expressions and posturing. While my whole family looked related with our short statures, golden blonde hair, and eyes that shaded between light brown and olive green, the Somnus King and Queen couldn't be more different from one another. King Reo had black hair, dark brown eyes, and stood a whole head taller than my dad while Queen Reo was sandy blonde (no hints of red like my family's version of blonde) with striking green eyes and a nimble frame. I imagined Emer growing up to look exactly like her, minus the queen's fidgeting.

"Forgive us, Your Highness," Queen Reo of Somnus said, her hands sliding down her skirts for the fourth time, "there has been a terrible misfortune."

My younger sister quietly scoffed behind us. "I knew I should have worn my lucky bracelet."

"Opal," I muttered, "I highly doubt your one little bracelet would have made a difference."

"How would you know, Dodo?" my identical twin, Ruby, jeered.

"Stop calling me that," I hissed back. "My name is Dot—with a T."

Technically, it was Peridot (named for my olive green eyes), but only Dad used my full name. Mom called me "Dainty Dot" for my frustrating tendency to be irritated by even my clothing seams.

Opal opened her mouth to contribute more to the bickering, but Dia turned around to give us a withering glare. It was one of those expressions that only our older sister could make. She had lots of practice between my siblings and me. Our brother, Cephas, simply stared off to the side, lost in some deep thought (probably about nothing).

I was glad that Ruby and Opal were silenced as the Somnus King bent his head close to Dad's and whispered, "We do not wish it to be widely known, but out of respect, I will inform you of our reason for canceling tonight's celebrations. Our daughter, Emerald, even your hostess, has fallen unconscious. We have our physician looking over her now and hope to resume the festivities by the morrow."

Emerald was unconscious? Of the many times I saw her at Noz Isle's midnight masquerades, her stamina had always impressed me. She danced nights away while many of us took breaks. What could cause her to lose consciousness on her sixteenth birthday?

My twin must have had the same concerns as she peeped out, "May we see Emer—ald? Princess Emerald, our hostess?"

Dia cleared her throat and added, "To pay respects and well wishes." She shot Ruby another warning glare, and I elbowed my twin.

Our parents had no knowledge of our friendships with the princesses of Somnus and even Huiess—enemies of our kingdom. They knew nothing about our midnight excursions to Noz Isle where we regularly met and danced without prejudices. For all they knew, Princess Emerald requested our presence simply because she wanted to invite all royalty of the Rezhina Valley. Our parents asked us to secret daggers beneath our gowns, expecting a skirmish between us. I resisted the urge to scratch at the metal blade at my calf. Scratching was inappropriate for a princess, but slanders, it was distracting.

Thankfully, my attention became refocused as Emer's youngest sister, Princess Tanzanite, approached from behind King and Queen Reo. She was a perfect mix of her parents with black stripes through her pale-blonde hair and brown-green eyes. Despite being only twelve years old (three years younger than Ruby and me), she was our same height, around a hundred and sixty centimeters. She wore a forest green dress with her hair left down. (Why did it feel like she kept secrets hidden under her hair?) I didn't need to be hyper sensitive to notice her exaggerated frantic posture. I flashed her a smile, but she kept her eyes on her parents. (Even if we hid our friendships, it seemed excessive to completely ignore us.) Her mom stepped away, asking if there was news about Emer's condition. Tanzi whispered something that made her mom frown and sneak glances at my parents.

"King and Queen Fashio," Queen Reo asked, "was there anyone else who joined your voyage from Ormio?"

"Of course," Dad said. "We brought our whole entourage."

"We have a witness claiming to have seen a man fleeing the room where Emer fell unconscious. He wore a black cloak with Ormio's symbol."

"Exactly what are you suggesting?" Dad asked, a hint of a growl in his voice. That was never a good sign.

"Is it possible that someone snuck onto your ship? Someone who might want to stir distrust between our kingdoms?"

"Is that what you feel?" Mom asked. "Distrust toward us?"

"Should we?" King Reo returned.

Queen Reo bounced her hands in a calming motion. "Please, let us not jump to conclusions. We will perform a thorough search of our castle. Meanwhile, I ask that you and your entire entourage retire to your guest chambers. We may assign a few guards to you for protection, if you wish."

"For whose protection?" Cephas muttered.

"What was that?" Dad snapped.

Cephas flinched before Dad's anger. Then my brother stood tall and faced the king. "If we aren't prisoners, then I prefer not to have guards."

"Agreed," Dad said. "We have our own guards. We do not need yours to spy on us."

"Please," Queen Reo said, "our only concern is for your safety."

"Veni, they deserve the truth," King Reo said, then returned to Dad. "Which is that we suspect someone in your entourage of malicious intent. We will have you escorted to your chambers, where you will stay for the remainder of the night or until the villain is found. Now, if you will excuse us, we have a search to coordinate."

The Queen of Somnus opened her mouth as if to say something to ease our treatment, but the king turned her away with a pivot. Princess Tanzi skipped after them (what a strangely perky walk for the depressing situation). I tried to get her attention again for some kind of message, but she never turned around.

Mom huffed and tossed her shawl over her shoulder. Four guards stepped around us, leading us to our chambers.

Within the click-clops of our footsteps, Ruby whispered, "What a disappointment."

"Truly," I muttered back. "I expected an argument between our parents, but I hoped to dance beside Emer and Pearl before our forced exit."

"I knew I should have worn my lucky bracelet," Opal murmured.

Dia flashed us a plotting smile over her shoulder. "Stop moping. The night is still young. We may find time with the others."

Indeed, we did. Dia petitioned for my sisters and me to share our own chamber, then managed to sneak notes to Garnet of Somnus and Ame of Huiess. We dismissed our chambermaids, insisting we'd manage our own bedding (after I received an extra mattress). Our solitude allowed us to arrange our mattresses for the optimal gathering space and secrecy when someone knocked on our door. It was Pearl. She ran in as a flash of perfectly black hair and a simple rose-pink gown to embrace each of us while Marin stood watch and Garnet looked over our sleeping guards. Tanzi ran in after Pearl, taking her own turn for hugs. (Maybe it was simply in comparison to Pearl's tenderness, but Tanzi's felt less than sincere.)

Dia smirked at Garnet. "You gave them one of your special sleeping potions? They work like charms."

"I can only hope," Garnet whispered, and shook her head of raven black hair, tied into a tight braid that circled like a crown. "How much do you know about the delay for Emer's ball?"

Dia shrugged. "Emer fell unconscious, and some witness claims Ormio's behind it. I can promise you, it wasn't anyone here. We all arrived with barely a second to breathe before we heard about Emer's fall."

Garnet glanced at Tanzi. "Our witness claims that someone from Ormio was seen before the incident."

Standing to her full height, Garnet approached Dia and sized her with her eyes. I had always thought Garnet was tall, though standing next to Dia, I realized they were about the same height. Dia was simply more rounded. Garnet's thinness suddenly seemed...stretched, spread thin, forced to stand taller, and straining from pressure.

She stared at Dia like trying to read a book in another language.

After an uncomfortable five seconds, she released a long breath. "We cannot afford distrust and secrets if we hope of finding the true culprit. I need your help."

Dia raised her eyebrows. "I could count on one hand how many times I've heard you say that. You must be desperate."

"Asking Ormio for help?" a new voice at the door said. "Definitely desperate."

Our attention turned to the Princesses of Huiess, Ame, Sapphire, and Toto. Like my family, the three of them looked like siblings with their matching dark brown hair, brown-spotted blue eyes, and bronze faces. Tanzi jumped straight to Sapphire with her biggest grin.

"Do you know what happened?" she asked.

Sapphire's expression went cloudy like she'd entered a dark daydream. "The purest green is consumed by black. She was always a sharp one, always on point."

Ame cleared her throat as she often did when Sapphire spoke in riddles. I truly wanted to see the younger princess in a match against the Riddle Maker one day.

"What's this," Ame asked, "about Emer's party delay? I say we have the party here and now. We have all the most important people. Except Emer, of course."

"Ooh," Tanzi exclaimed, "that sounds like a ball!"

"Hush, Tanzi," Garnet scolded her youngest sister. "We are mere walls away from others. Besides, dancing without Emer would feel wrong."

"What exactly happened to Emer?" I asked.

Pearl clamped her hands together and sniffled. "Oh, it was absolutely awful. Emer was—we can tell them, right?"

Tanzi pointed an accusatory finger at my sisters and me. "They already know. They made it happen."

"Did not!" Ruby shouted back.

"We know nothing," Dia said, annoyed. "This suspect with Ormio's crest is not in league with us."

Ame frowned, and Toto reached for her side dagger (at least, I assumed it was a dagger hidden in that pouch, based on the size and shape). "Someone from Ormio attacked Emer?"

"Stop," Garnet said, raising her voice, her chest heaving with quick breaths. "Tanzi saw someone mysterious fleeing the scene of the crime before Emer entered, though we have no idea who hurt Emer or if Emer was even the initial target. Pointing fingers will only make matters worse. We need to be together more than ever. Which is why I will share what happened. We will be strong and fight this unknown together."

Tanzi pouted. "But I saw the attacker. He wore an Ormio crest."

Garnet shot her a withering glare that seemed more tired than Dia's earlier stare at Opal, Ruby, and me.

"Fine," Tanzi muttered, then whined, "But what if telling them everything makes our parents or others discover our secret friendships? They would misunderstand our bonds and force us apart. Everyone must make an oath that what we discuss together will stay only among us."

She met each of our gazes to confirm our conviction. We each responded in turn to keep this secret.

"Very well," Garnet said. "Marin, you were first on the scene. Tell us what happened."

Marin talked about her day, starting with delivering the Ormio wine to the kitchens, and seeing Emer flustered, but alive and well. Then, a shout from the corridor. Emer was down on the floor by the spinning wheel. Poisoned.

"Our physician is still examining her," Marin said. "We hope that as soon as he can determine the poison, he may determine the antidote and save Emer. Then, we may continue her festivities as planned."

Tanzi whimpered, "What if the physician cannot determine the poison? Even if he does, what if he cannot make the antidote in time?"

Garnet stared hard at her youngest sister. "I refuse to consider that as an option. He will have time."

Slanders, it was difficult not to admire her confidence. She would make a powerful queen.

Tanzi opened her mouth to whine more, but Garnet continued, "My strongest theory is that whoever poisoned Emer, whether it was on purpose or accident, whether they were from Ormio or not, did it to divide us. Why else would they wear a cloak with Ormio's crest? Anyone clever enough to go through our castle undetected would be clever enough to wear a disguise. Whoever poisoned Emer wants us to suspect and distrust each other. That is why I say that now, more than ever, we need to stay strong. We need to stay together. If Emer is healed tonight, but we lose faith in one another, then the culprit has still won. I refuse to let some sneaky little person filled with hate to be the victor over me—to be a wedge between my friends and me. What about you?"

While Tanzi pouted with unspoken disagreements, Dia gave Ame a determined look. Ame smirked back.

"Huiess takes pride in our sneaky and clever people, but whoever poisoned Emer was sloppy. He let himself get caught and didn't backup his plan. I cannot speak for my parents, but I want to help. Sapphire, Toto?"

Toto nodded, and Sapphire tilted her head sideways. "Rezhina needs to be united, no matter the cost." Could that girl ever say something without sounding creepy?

"We too," Dia said. "You all know I have no taste for war. Knowledge is a far greater strength than any muscle. When my turn comes to rule Ormio, I want our kingdoms to learn and build together."

"Hear, hear," I said, raising an imaginary glass.

"Words," Ruby cursed. "That was what I was going to say. How do you always steal the words out of my mouth?"

"Maybe because we're twins, but I'd never speak of The Words in vain." I finished by sticking out my tongue at her. She responded with her usual air-pinch as if to catch my extended tongue (at least her smirk spoke of teasing).

Opal puffed out her young chest. "We stand with you. I'll wear every single one of my lucky pieces of jewelry, just in case."

Sapphire whispered, "If only luck stood a chance against the divining stars."

I inwardly groaned. Here, we were trying to support each other, and Sapphire had to bring up Huiess's debatable religion? Thankfully, Garnet took control of the conversation again.

"Thank you, everyone. I have a feeling that tensions might be tight for the next few days. I hoped we could use this evening ball to push our parents into creating a solution, but this gathering has been far more satisfying. I trust you. You are more than friends to me. You are my sisters."

She smiled at each of us, but my eyes wandered to her real sisters. Marin nodded solemnly, Pearl beamed with happiness, and Tanzi…looked irritated.

Somehow, despite our strengthened bonds that night, I knew the tests of those bonds were only beginning.

Chapter 2

EMER

One hundred years later, Emer sat with her recently awakened sisters. The morning after waking Pearl was almost like old times to Emer. She sat at a fireplace hearth, enjoying a breakfast of warm ham and eggs and listening to her younger sister Pearl sing a sweet melody. Her older sister Marin sat with her husband, Ranae, on a side bench, smiling softly while snacking on whole berries.

In some ways, it was better than the days before Emer's hundred-harvest slumber. Emer also had a hand to hold as Prince Caden Seaver of Uldra sat beside her. Framed within his strong jawline and inky black hair, he smiled at her with light blue eyes that reminded her of their love confessions and passionate kisses.

Prince Mica Wright of the fallen Zubra Kingdom sat closest to Pearl, staring at her like she was an angel. Emer had to admit, she looked the part. Her younger sister literally glowed, especially when her brown eyes met Mica's. She wore a simple pink kirtle dress that complemented her straight black hair. Not even sleeping for a hundred harvests could give her bed-head.

In other ways, however, the scene was too different to compare to the old days. Instead of sitting around one of the many grand fireplaces within the stone castle of Somnus, they sat in a small plastered house in the middle of the Midnight Forest. Instead of her sisters Garnet and Tanzi accompanying them, they had new friends.

Prince Leo Bahr of the fallen Braeder Kingdom stood like a giant thundercloud of brown hair and light brown eyes against the back wall. Prince Shinópu Chushiama of the fallen Chafan Kingdom of dwarves sat motionlessly on his knees near the wooden door with his thin black ponytail and dual-swords crossing his back. He gained his freedom two weeks ago, but he still acted like a humble slave of Charlotte, the ogress. At least Emer's friend Jesse and her dwarf husband, Thachuma, seemed more jovial from escaping Charlotte's servitude as they took a break from cooking to dance with Pearl's songs. Their newest friend and host, Hanzo, could compete with Mica's focus on Pearl, acting unsure and awkward around the rest of the company.

While Emer was happy to have these new friends, she worried about her missing sisters and past friends. They still needed to find Garnet, recruit an army, and save the northern grassland kingdoms from the ogres. According to Pearl, to find Garnet, they needed to follow her steps into Ormio. The twin princesses, Ruby and Peridot, were their next clues to finding the rightful heir and defense against Queen Tanzi's rule.

Pearl finished her song, and everyone clapped. Even Leo clapped a few times before settling into his usual scowl and opening his mouth.

Here we go again, Emer mentally sighed, expecting Leo's usual tirade about going back to Uldra to fight the ogres, despite their lack of army or resources.

"I propose we set off before the sun is high," he said. "Princesses Ruby and Peridot can't wait forever."

Emer dropped her knife and jaw. Caden looked up with wide, blinking eyes.

"Er, Leo?" Mica asked. "I'm all for this change of heart thing, but are you hypnotized?"

Leo snarled. "If anyone tried playing with my head, they'd find a stone wall mentality and an arrow in their gut."

Caden muttered, "That's Leo alright." Speaking louder, he asked, "What changed your mind about searching for the princesses?"

Leo stared at Caden and ground his teeth. "You didn't give me much of a choice. I'm either stuck with you fools, or I return to Uldra to fight the ogres alone and empty-handed. You're all content to chase legends while our people are slaughtered, but what else can I do about it?"

Caden met his scowl. "I'm far from content with our people's situation, but we need more support and renewed energy to beat the ogres."

"As you've said," Leo growled. "If waking all these beshrewed princesses is what it takes, then the faster the better."

As much as Emer appreciated his shifting sides, she had to add, "Waking the princesses is only step one. Step two is to make the people aware of our return and acknowledge our authority. Then, step three will be convincing them to join us in our campaign against the ogres in the north, despite their queen's neutrality in the issue."

"I may be able to help with that."

Emer and the others turned to the speaker. Hanzo. The hunting dwarf was the last of his family, left to watch over Pearl through the generations of her cursed sleep, trapped within the Midnight Forest his whole life.

He bowed first to Pearl, then to Prince Shinópu before speaking. "I kept my family's oath to watch

Princess Pearl while she slept. Now that the darkness is gone and Princess Pearl is awake, I would like to leave this forest. I would like to meet others and tell them your story. I will say how you came to my family for help, how Queen Tanzanite came in disguise as an old woman to poison Princess Pearl, how Princess Garnet put her to sleep and escaped, then how you all came to save us."

Pearl gave him a sad smile. "Are you sure you do not want to join us as we search for the other princesses?"

The young dwarf's face flashed through a couple of expressions, including elation and fear. Settling on gratitude, he said, "Thank you, but after living alone for many harvests, I will travel best alone, I think."

"If you insist," Pearl said. "I wish there was something we could give you to thank you for your family's lifelong sacrifice."

Caden nodded. "In fact, a token from the princesses might solidify his story as he spreads the word of your awakening."

Emer frowned. "What could we give him? Our possessions were lost with time. All we have are the clothes on our backs and—" She cut off as an idea came to mind. She gestured for everyone to follow her outside. Glancing at the fruit bushes that surrounded the cabin, she asked Hanzo, "Do you have a favorite fruit?"

He pointed at a clump of orange berries that grew low to the ground like herbs. "The shortberries are the most versatile and I like their tart flavor."

"Perfect." Emer asked a nearby forest fern to weave a basket with its leaves. She plucked it away, filled it halfway with dirt, then went to the shortberries. "Will you allow me to replant a portion of you into this basket? This man favors you above all others, and I would like for him to take you on his travels."

Hanzo stared in wonder as Emer replanted a small section with a dozen berries into the basket, then sprinkled more dirt to cover the roots.

"Now," she said to the repotted shortberries, "I have a great favor to ask of you. Whenever he picks one of your berries, I want you to regrow that berry during the day before the sun sets. I want you to regrow your berries once a day, every day, until I give you different directions. Can you do that?"

The plant shivered with excitement about the challenge.

Marin sighed. "That poor plant will soak away its nutrients far too fast. Hanzo, may I borrow your water jug?"

Hanzo nodded and led the group back indoors as he retrieved a glass jar. Marin took it in her hands and

20

stared hard at it. "I have no idea if this will work," she muttered, then spoke loudly. "Moisture in the air, pure water that surrounds us and gives us life, gather into this jar until it is full. As long as this man carries this jar, make sure it is filled every sunrise and sunset."

As she spoke, droplets of water began to grow inside the jar until they became too heavy and slid to the bottom. There was a whole tablespoon's worth by the time she finished her instructions.

"How fascinating," Pearl said. "Mica told me of Emer's power with plants, but I had not expected to see it in Somnus. And, Marin! You can command water? How marvelous! May I contribute?"

Emer watched, curious what her youngest sister could do—other than glow when she was happy.

"Please," Pearl said to Hanzo, "do you have a favorite lantern? I would like to light it."

Hanzo went to the fireplace mantle to retrieve a small lantern with a top handle for carrying. He handed it to Pearl.

"How wonderful," Pearl said. "Lucy, may you appear in Somnus?"

"Lucy?" Emer asked right before a small ball of light appeared in front of Pearl's face.

"Beshrews!" Ranae stepped back while Leo cursed with, "Demons of the South!"

Mica's face opened like hearing a forgotten favorite song. "It's just like my dream."

"Lucy!" Pearl cried for joy. Her skin glowed again as she beamed with happiness. "Please duplicate yourself and sit in this lantern so that it may never dim and forever provide light to this loyal dwarf."

Emer gaped. "You can create light?"

"And you named it Lucy?" Marin added.

Caden chuckled as he finished another note on his parchment roll. "It's fitting. They called Princess Pearl the Light of Somnus, after all."

Emer smirked back. "That nickname had been inspired by her charity and love towards others. Not for literally glowing."

Hanzo gaped through the whole demonstration of magic and bowed low to the floor. "Thank you. Thank you! I-I cannot…How can I repay you?"

Pearl touched his shoulder, bidding him to rise. "You watched over me all your life. This is simply my attempt to repay you."

"However," Emer added, "you would immensely help us if you spread the word of our awakening and petition to help the grassland kingdoms. Please, tell the people how we plan to wake the others and restore our kingdoms to their former glory."

Caden unrolled his map of the Rezhina Valley to show Hanzo. Pointing at the Midnight Forest, he said,

"We're here. You'll find the largest congregations of people beside the mountains. I suggest you travel northward, then curve eastward, towards Uldra. We need the people aware of the ogre situation up north so that they may help us when needed."

"Ogres?" Hanzo asked. "You mean that creature that followed you into the glade?"

"Yes," Thachuma pitched in. Their loyal cook and friend bowed before Caden. His wife, Jesse, joined his side. "If we may, Prince Seaver, we'd like to join Hanzo. We will testify of the ogres' brutality and your means of rescuing us."

"Jesse?" Emer reached for her friend. Jesse knew next to nothing of their friendship in England, but they'd bonded during their captivity under the ogress, Charlotte. "Whatever will we do without you?"

Jesse smiled sadly. "I first joined this misadventure to provide services and the necessary feminine touch to keep the princes from accidentally diseasing themselves. I believe you and your sisters more than fill their needs."

"Also," Thachuma added, "I believe our services will be of better use helping this oaf—" he gestured at Hanzo "—to integrate with society and spread the word. We need an army to beat the ogres. The word of three humble servants should be more convincing than the word of a single hermit."

Hanzo frowned, but Caden laughed. "You have my blessing to leave. I trust your accounts of the tale to be true. Though it might help to have a document signed by each of us."

"With our seals," Mica said, rotating a ring on his right hand.

Emer retrieved another piece of parchment from Caden's dwindling stash. Before handing it to Prince Seavers, she demanded, "Write small."

He smirked. "I'll try." Switching out his usual smudgeable charcoal for a quill and ink jar, he wrote with careful calligraphy. He penned a brief explanation about his travels through Somnus with his fellow princes, seeking the princesses of old for aid in their plight against the ogres. He declared their awakening and their united hopes to cleanse their kingdoms of the ogres and tyranny. He signed it, then stamped his seal ring beside his signature. Mica, Leo, and Shinópu signed below, then Emer signed in a new column.

Marin gave it an approving nod before signing, then handed it to her husband to sign as the former Admiral of the Somnus Navy. Pearl signed last, lightly blowing on the ink to dry.

"With that," Marin said, "we become official traitors to the crown of Queen Tanzi."

Chapter 3

DOT

I woke to the setting of the scariest stories ever told; alone in the woods in the dark of night.

I lay on my back, staring up at dead pine trees and scattered clouds across the night sky. The full moon hung low on the mountainous horizon. Welcome to the darkest hours of the night before the sunrise.

The scariest part of all was the scream. It continued without ending or changing pitch, ringing through my ears and silencing all else.

Wind caressed my face, tilting the dead trees, but no creaking or groaning escaped them.

An annoying bump on my back encouraged me to sit up. Why didn't the leaves crinkle beneath my movement? Why didn't the wind howl? Why didn't the branches rustle?

Spirits of Slanderous Words. The screaming in my head was literally deafening.

An owl took flight above me without a hoot or woosh through its wings. Despite the terror of everything else around me, the silent majesty of the owl was actually peaceful. My heart lightened marginally.

If the constant scream was the scariest part, then the weirdest part was my clothing. I wore a shirt and trousers like a man and the warriors of Huiess. The shirt cropped above my hips with an overcoat that opened in the front and was made of strange glossy material. My footwear was also made of more layers than leather, with a strong sole and laces on top. At least these scanty clothes were comfortable and flexible if I needed to run for my life.

With no other options in sight, I stood, hoping to gain a better perspective of my surroundings. Where was I? Somewhere in Ormytha Forest? No, Ormthya's trees had flat leaves that changed colors in the fall. These spiky trees grew in the forests of Somnus. What had I been doing out here? Why was I alone? I rarely went anywhere without my twin sister.

A little wooden post directed me to a nearby trail. The dirt path between the grasses had many large rocks, forcing me to keep my eyes on my feet. Rolling a cart over this worn path would be unpleasant, to say the least. Having no idea which way to go, I chose the direction away from the mountains. If I was anywhere in Rezhina Valley, walking away from the mountains would take me toward the lake and cities. Based on the coniferous trees and the sun's direction, I supposed that I was somewhere on the western side of Somnus.

A vague memory of following Crown Princess Garnet of Somnus through the woods slipped through my mind, but it was gone as quickly as it came. The memory had felt recent and also distant, like a yesterday that felt a week old.

Searching my memories for something more recent, I remembered finding sanctuary with Garnet. A little inn. It was a family favorite, and the innkeepers recognized me. They had a running joke because of my sensitivity and arranged my bedding with a pile of a dozen mattresses. Despite the stack of mattresses, I remembered tossing and turning, unable to sleep from some lump in the bed. It had been as irritating as the pebble in my shoe.

I stood on one foot to take off my shoe and dumped it upside-down. Nothing fell out, but the pebble somehow moved to my other shoe. I set my foot down, and the lump returned to my dominant foot.

Slanders! It was the lump from the bed! I could still feel it in this…dream!

I analyzed my surroundings with new insight. If I was dreaming, that could explain why I was alone in this unfamiliar place.

Hiking alone in the woods at night was never the start to a pleasant dream. Was I supposed to take light steps with little noise, or heavy steps with lots of noise? Light steps would keep me undetected by humans in wait, but loud steps would frighten away any animals. As if I could hear them beyond the screaming in the first place (it helped not to focus on the sound). I eventually distracted myself enough to tune out the ringing pitch, and the dream became silent as feathers.

I met no one during my nervous and limped walk but passed several signs of humanity (posts with numbers, a small bridge over a stream, and even wooden stairs when the path grew steep). At least I spotted a few more curious night birds on the hunt, calming my nerves, if only a little.

To my great relief, I found a wider path as the sky lightened with the promise of a sunrise.

There was something different about this road. It was paved with some smooth and solid black sand instead of cobblestone or dirt. There weren't any buildings nearby. What kind of kingdom was so wealthy to build roads outside of cities? It was also painted with yellow and white lines. I knew of no such roads in all the kingdoms of Rezhina Valley.

I continued to walk down the gradual slope, away from the mountains as the sun slowly peeked above the horizon. I frowned as I realized that the sun wasn't the reason for the growing light ahead of me. My shadow stretched in the wrong direction.

Turning around, I found two white lights glaring at me. They belonged to a large beast that charged down the road.

My mouth opened and breath escaped me with an inaudible scream. I ran the other direction and off of the road. (Slanders, that pebble hurt and made me limp with every step!) I ran, panting as the lights grew stronger and brighter around me. Then my shadow disappeared as the light pulled ahead of me. It stayed on the road, but kept pace with me. (What kind of creature would do that?) With the lights no longer blinding me, I noticed movement on the beast.

A part of it opened, sliding down, revealing…a woman inside.

She stared at me with wide eyes and pursed lips of worry. Her long brown hair was braided into a single tail that draped down her shoulder. She waved at me and gestured for me to come closer. Not likely. Even if she looked genuinely concerned and vaguely familiar. How did I know her?

Her mouth moved, but I heard nothing. I tried to tell her, "I cannot hear you," but only blurred moans vibrated among the high pitch in my head. Using both hands, she began to make shapes and signs. I had never seen such sign language before, yet I somehow understood it.

"D-O-T," she spelled out my name. "Can I help you?" She signed the entire question with a single gesture, placing a thumbs-up on her other palm, then sliding it from herself to me with high eyebrows and a pinched mouth. A yes or no question.

How did I know that? Even more peculiar, how did I know how to answer?

Like playing a flute piece with my eyes closed, my hands and fingers knew what to do. I rubbed my palm in a circular motion over my heart. "Please."

She waved for me to come closer again. She offered to help, and she knew my name. If this was a trap, it was a very convincing one. I stepped closer to the beast with its bright white lights up front and glaring red lights in the back.

The woman pointed to her right, showing me an empty seat beside her. I walked around the back of the beast and found a latch on the side. Not a beast after all, but a carriage. (How did it move without horses?)

I let myself in. The woman also wore trousers and a glossy overcoat that cut off around her hips. She frowned at me with concerned eyes.

"Are you OK?" she signed.

OK. Like the sign language itself, the slang translated in my mind. "No," I signed back. "I'm not

OK. I'm tired. Scared. Confused. You know my name. How? I'm deaf. Why? I know sign language. How?"

She slowly lowered her hands in front of her chest, palms down. "Calm down. Breathe. You're safe now. Tell me what happened?"

I released a heavy breath. Why was I out in the woods? What had happened?

The woman asked, "Why are you alone? Where's Leo?"

The last sign hadn't been spelled out, but again, I somehow knew the name. The sign had started like the sign for "lion," like a claw combing back its hair from its forehead. Then it shifted into an "L" shape with the thumb pointed at her ear. It was my sign name for Leo. I had given it to him.

Memories of another life flooded me. I remembered meeting a tall man with broad shoulders and long thick hair that covered most of his face. I remembered his light brown eyes and the way they smiled at me. Leo was hard of hearing with about sixty percent audio. He had blown out his hearing during a hunting accident when a gun backfired.

What was a gun? How did I know exactly what it was without knowing anything about it?

More importantly, who was Leo? How did I know everything about him without knowing him? He was two and a half years older than I was, recently graduated, and had left town for a summer job. He had left me. But he had left with a promise. He left to earn money…for us.

I looked down at my left hand, noticing for the first time a small band of metal around my ring finger. It had a single small peridot in the center.

This dream made me engaged to a stranger.

Looking back to the woman, another onslaught of memories (fewer and smaller, thankfully) told me that she was one of my school translators. Ms. Hill. She had learned American Sign Language while serving for her church then went to university to become an English teacher. Ms. Hill often exaggerated her signs and didn't feel comfortable signing while driving, leaving me to simply wonder while traveling at the speed of the elusive Ormytha unicorn.

The beastly vehicle slowed in front of a large house with lights beside the door. Moving a lever, Ms. Hill freed her hands to sign, "Your mom's inside. She's worried about you. Talk with her?"

I released a slow breath, then wiggled my fist up and down. "Yeah."

I stepped out of the strange carriage, analyzing it again as my teacher waved goodbye and put it into motion. How did the beastly thing move? Maybe I could add it to my long list of questions to ask my mom.

Turning back to the house, I found nothing familiar…yet somehow it was all familiar. How did I know this was my home? How did I know my mom laid these stones leading to the front door by herself? How did I know the large building behind the house was my mom's workshop, where she made wooden furniture and sculptures for locals and seasonal tourists? How did I know the un-flickering torch lights beside the door were fueled by electricity?

Maybe it was a side effect of the dream. Things somehow made sense in dreams.

I walked into the house without a key, opening my view to a large room separated only by a long counter between the kitchen and everything else. The main area was furnished with beautifully crafted wooden benches with thick cushions. Between them was a low table covered with books and mugs. There was a circle of windows leading to the back where two chairs sat beside a round table. Somehow, I knew that my mom made all the furniture in the house.

The woman herself sat in the middle room with her head in her hands, her elbows on her knees. She looked exactly like the Queen of Ormio (same golden hair, light brown eyes, and loving face), save for her simple trousers (jeans?) and cropped undershirt (T-shirt?). Unfortunately, I recognized her position of despair. She looked like that after every lost battle against Huiess.

As soon as I walked in, her face popped up, then her eyes went directly to my hand. When she spotted the ring, she turned away and hid her face.

She knew to look for it. Leo had asked Mom for permission to marry me. She had allowed it, hoping I'd say no.

Why had I said yes?

Peeping around her disappointment, Mom noticed my tear-stained eyes.

"Dorothy!" She signed my name with a "D" then poked a "dot" in the air, but mouthed the full name. My full name was Peridot, not Dorothy. Who was Dorothy?

Unfortunately, my confusion only worried my mom more. "What happened? Are you OK?"

"No," I signed. I thought about telling her about my deafness, the persistent pebble under my foot, my dreaming state, and my actual name. Somehow, I knew my mom wouldn't understand my confusion. Besides, she was more concerned about the ring on my hand. I signed, "Leo's gone."

"Gone?" she repeated, then asked cautiously, "For work?"

I nodded. It was a legitimate reason, but why did it still hurt like I'd been abandoned?

Mom took me into her arms and held me. I cried and soaked in her warmth. She waited a whole minute for my wiggling to end the embrace.

"You said 'yes?'" she asked with questioning eyebrows.

Thrown into this storyline, I shrugged and wiped at my tears. The ring scratched my face. Ouch. That would take some getting used to.

"I know," Mom signed, "you love Leo, and he said he'll wait until after your graduation to marry...but that's still two years away. That's a long time to be engaged. You could make other friends, date other people—"

"Why?" I asked, reviewing the memories that I had of Leo. "Leo loves me. He's committed to me, he respects me, and he works hard. What more do you want?"

Truly, to find such a prince in Ormio would have been a dream come true.

Mom's shoulders slumped with a heavy sigh. "I know. But...you're so very young," she signed, emphasizing "young."

I pouted. "You and dad were how old when you married?"

"That's not fair," she signed. "The town was smaller back then, and we didn't have the internet to broaden our world. And look what happened."

Divorce. The thought slammed into me and made me want to cry. Even if it was just a dream, the thought of my parents separating hurt too much.

A second despair hit me as I realized that Dorothy had no siblings. As much as my brother and sisters irritated me at times, their sudden absence created a gaping hole in my heart.

Seeing my pain, Mom reluctantly circled her fist around her chest. "Sorry, but I don't want the same thing to happen to you. I know, right now you think you'll always love Leo no matter what, but love changes. Use this time while Leo's in Texas to learn about yourself and go on your own adventures."

Psh. Parents and their annoying habit to limit teenagers' capabilities. I was almost sixteen. Dorothy had been limited by her hearing loss, but that hadn't stopped her from experiencing life. I had vague memories of socializing, exercising, learning, and developing love. If anything, I had memories of working harder than everyone else to experience the same things. Shouldn't that prove my capabilities to dedicate myself and accomplish my goals, whatever they were?

Without my siblings to talk to and ask for direction, my mind turned to Leo for support. I loved my mom, but I needed a conversation with a best friend.

Rather than respond to my mom's worries, I asked, "You know where Leo went for work? How far away will he be? When can I see him?" Like the muscle memory that taught me sign language, somehow I knew that seeing Leo would give me answers about this strange dream.

Mom's shoulders slumped again. "He's working in Texas, right? Give him some time to travel and settle into his work and new home."

"His home is here," I signed, pouting my lips. Too annoyed to continue the conversation, I went to the kitchen, leaving my mom disappointed. Not like it was the first time.

I was terribly tired from the morning hike, but my dissatisfied stomach spread its irritation through my body. Relying on the strange subconscious awareness of where and what everything was, I grabbed a bowl and prepared myself a serving of grainy chunks drowned in milk (cereal?). The sugary wheat and cold milk helped wake me—scratch that—helped make me more alert of my surroundings and situation.

Mom prepared herself a bowl, but didn't try to pick up the conversation again. Good. My hands were busy holding my bowl and spoon anyway (what a convenient excuse to avoid talking).

After eating, I went to my bedroom to…check notifications? Some mental habit wanted to know if Leo had posted anything. On what? Was there some kind of town board where people posted job offers, market times, and Wanted posters? My dream said there was, but I couldn't determine how to gain access to it from my bedroom. Maybe it was in one of the many books that lined two shelves on the wall?

I leafed through a couple of them, discovering their wealth of knowledge on birds from places I'd never heard of. I studied the many colorful pictures, amazed at their detail and information. The book labeled as "Washington" was the most worn with dog-eared corners and curled pages. A bookmark with the quote, "Home is where the heart is," was stuck in the pages about the Washington Cascade mountain range. Yes, this was my dream's home.

Fascinating as the read was, the uncomfortable lump distracted me as it rotated to whichever spot I rested the most weight. I eventually laid down to disperse my weight as evenly as possible, making it easier to ignore the lump under my shoulder. I read book after book until exhaustion turned into sleep.

When I "woke," it was still daylight, and still in Washington. I looked out my window to spot a red

"OPEN" light shining by the door of my mom's workshop. I had heard of mushrooms that glowed in the dark, but that sign was like a rope of embers. Magical as the sign was, it was simply my mom's way to tell me and her customers that she was working inside.

I grabbed a couple of my books and went out to join her. Her hands were too busy with the dangerous and fascinating machinery to talk. She wore earmuffs, and I grabbed my own pair because, "being deaf doesn't mean your ears can't be damaged." I watched her work, then sat on a large ball-like cushion that molded to my body. I had a feeling that this was my spot where I frequently sat and read while Mom worked. Despite the seat's cushioning and no matter my positioning, I felt that irritating lump beneath me.

The day passed in silence (when I tuned out the never-ending high pitch), and I found myself more easily sucked into books without sounds to distract me. I yearned for the words to take my mind off of the constant scream and my physical and emotional pain. I read about the fascinating birds and places to visit in Washington, then grabbed my book on Texas (the place Leo had gone to work). There wasn't a page on his exact location since he was working in a rural area outside the cities, but I still had several pages dog-eared in the mid-west part of the state.

Apparently, Texas was several hundred miles away from Washington, but still in the same country. Slanders, this dream was huge! Through some confusing trials and errors, I discovered how to use a device called "my phone" to view maps. I found a map of the United States of America, then traced the roads between me and Leo. My initial impressions of this dream-country's size were overwhelming. Lake Imazhin was perhaps the size of a Great Lake, and this country had five of them tucked in an upper corner!

A couple of days later, I was reading over a book about Utah with its map beside me. I lay on my stomach since feeling the lump under my ribs was currently more comfortable than feeling it on my shoulder blade or posterior. Mom sat beside me with enough heft to shake the floor.

"What's this?" she signed.

"A map," I signed, lamely.

She rolled her eyes. "Southern Utah? You're interested in the National Parks?"

"Utah is between us and Leo."

Mom leaned back. "You want to meet him there? Dot, I don't know if he can travel away from his summer job."

"No. I want to go see Leo in Texas. Going through Utah is the fastest."

"You want to go to Texas?" She waved at me to hand over my phone. Pinching her fingers on the screen and tapping a few times, she looked back up with high brows. "That's a thirty-hour drive. You got your driver's permit three months ago, and now you want to take a road trip? Do you know the permit laws in Oregon, Utah, or Texas? They're all different, you know?"

Oh, they were? I'd learned to drive a horse-carriage after my tenth harvest. Driving a machine couldn't be harder than driving a living-breathing-opinionated animal…could it?

Mom puffed up her cheeks and blew them out in a long breath, shaking her head. "I know the day Leo left was hard. You changed."

I answered with a mere pinch of my mouth and shrug. That was the day this dream began. I had no idea what I was like before (who *Dorothy* was) other than I looked the same and had been deeply in love with Leo.

"I can't stop you?" she asked. Her expression said that she already knew the answer.

"Nope," I signed.

Her shoulders lowered dramatically with a heavy sigh. "You mule mule." No, that wasn't right. I re-translated it as, "You stubborn mule." A memory flashed through my mind as I recognized the inside

41

joke. She laughed at "stubborn" and "mule" having the same sign, and I always responded the same; "Like Dad."

She smiled sadly and nodded.

"I'm ahead of schedule for my seasonal pieces, but I need to give my contractors at least one week's notice before I drive halfway across the country with my daughter. Can you wait that long?"

I nodded. I'd already spent a few days in this dream, and the depth of its details led me to believe I'd continue to dream at least until I saw Leo again.

Chapter 4

RUBY

Was there anything more confusing than being eaten whole by an old woman? One minute, I was helping the lonely granny with setting breakfast, then the next, she was chasing me around her little cottage with a ferocity and spryness too strange for her old body. She cornered me in the bedroom, leaping at me with nails—no, claws! and teeth—no, fangs! baring at me.

At the last second, I recognized my attacker. I had once called her my friend at many Noz Isle masquerades. She was a wolf in sheep's clothing.

Fear and confusion distorted my memory. Why would my friend pretend to be an old woman? Why would she attack me? No, she was a wolf. She had to be. As darkness swallowed me, it only made sense that I'd been eaten. The darkness was deeper than a forest during a moonless night, more than my bedchamber after the fire burned out, worse than the bottom boat deck with no lantern. Those places had familiarity. Those places had objects to gauge my position. No, this darkness was empty like the bottom of a starving wolf's stomach. I saw nothing, and it was warm.

I drifted through sleep. No light, movement, or hunger measured the time that passed. I simply rocked back and forth like a babe in the womb.

My unseen surroundings pressed in around me, growing warmer. Somewhere in the distance, I thought I heard panting, like a dog in a sprint. I wiggled through the darkness, unsure which direction would take me away from the animal. I turned left, right, up, down. It made no difference. The heat increased and the dog became more agitated. It whined, growled, barked, then—

Howl.

I sat up in my bed, panting as if I had been the dog. Unfortunately, ending the dream gave me no comfort. I felt the blankets around me, the mattress below, the light gown around my body…but the empty darkness had followed me into reality.

I blinked, but saw nothing. There was a warm area on my skin, coming from the right. I looked that way, hoping to find a light. Nothing.

A dog barked in the distance, and I yelped in fright.

Hurried footsteps pounded across wooden flooring, coming closer. The screech of a door announced someone entering my sleeping chamber.

"Biddy! Are you alright? What are you still doing in bed at this hour?"

"I—" I hesitated, wondering if the man was truly speaking to me. It sounded like Dad, the King of Ormio. Except, what had he called me? Biddy? What an odd nickname. Choosing to focus on his last question, I asked, "What hour is it?"

"It's eight o'clock. The chickens must be hungry if you've been in bed all morning."

Eight? How was it still dark? I rubbed my eyes clear of their morning stiffness as the horror of reality hit me.

I was blind.

My burst of tears encouraged Dad to take pity on me and feed the chickens for me. Apparently, it was Sunday and his day off from overseeing work on our cotton farm.

My tears continued through the whole morning. I couldn't be blind. I couldn't be on a farm. I couldn't feed the chickens. Someone had ruined my sight and played a horrid prank on me, calling me Biddy.

Where was the rest of my family? When would they shout, "Surprise!" and make it all better? We frequently teased and played pranks on each other, but never to this extent. They were cunning enough for something this elaborate (especially Dia), but too kind for something this cruel.

My stomach began to complain, and Dad came in. He sat next to me on my bed, then took my hand, gently guiding me to the tray of food he brought.

"The doctors said this would happen," Dad said, rubbing my back. I hardly appreciated the simple scratching before, but now, I leaned into it, yearning for more evidence that he was there. "They said the difficulty of being blind will come and go in waves. You've been so good these past few years, coping with your accident. It's natural and okay to relapse into the fear as long as you come out stronger. I'm here for you."

Images flashed across my mind: a massive green machine reaping the cotton harvest faster than a dozen men, Dad shouting at me to "Get back!" then…pain across my face.

How did I have those memories? Why did all this make sense, even though none of it could be real?

Understanding hit me like a slap. I was dreaming.

In that case, all I had to do was wake up. I pinched myself, but remained where I was. Thinking of times I woke up after failing to eat a stolen biscuit, I put a spoonful of some thick cream into my mouth. Whoa! Vanilla exploded across my tongue with a sweetness that was smoother than sugar. With the taste and texture came an unknown name: pudding. How was this a dream? I had never eaten in my dreams before, and I couldn't have come up with that flavor or funny name. What was this place?

Dad left me alone to take the dishes away. A little whine and quick sniffing entered my room.

"Words!" I cursed. What was a dog doing in my bedroom? Had I snuck one away again?

Light paws stepped around my room then a wet nose nudged my hand. A memory and concept wedged itself into my mind like other facets of this dream life.

I had a…seeing-eye dog? As if I was some mythical heroine who received help from animals? I'd heard tales of such highly trained animals from the courts of Braeder, but had considered them more fictional than true. Mom had seeded the doubt deep into my mind, knowing that if they were true, little to nothing would stop me from wanting one as a pet.

Apparently, it was true in this dream.

I slid my hand over the dog's head to scratch behind his ears. The fur on his face and the top of his head was like a rabbit's: short and incredibly soft. Soft enough to impact my hard and heavy heart. His neck was covered like a mane with longer fur but equally soft. It thinned under his belly and became coarse around his rear as I scratched him all over.

"Good boy," I said, sniffling back my tears. Just as I instinctively knew it was a male, I knew his name too. "Good, Rayban."

He helped me see, so naturally, I named him after a popular brand for eye-glasses. Yep. I was unsure where the random information came from, but some things made more sense in dreams than in reality.

I pet Rayban, rubbed his belly, and asked him to come up on the bed to nap with me. I got the sense that Dad wouldn't be happy with Rayban on my bed, but I wanted him within reach and was tired from crying. I drifted back to sleep, but woke with my eyes still blind and my arms still wrapped around the fluffy dog.

Taking a note from Dia, I made a list of pros and cons about this dream. Cons: being blind and missing my mom and siblings. Pros: tasty foods and a faithful dog. Dogs were living proof of good in the world, so maybe this dream wasn't the worst place ever.

Carefully feeling my way out of bed, I explored my bedroom, finding an oddly familiar walking stick within reach. I didn't use it as I felt my way around the edges of the room, impressed by the carved curves of the wooden nightstand, confused by a door that led to a walk-in closet, then surprised by the recognition

I felt as I touched each piece of clothing, somehow knowing exactly how each one fit on me.

Back into the room, I bumped into another wooden table—no, a desk. I opened the drawers filled with glass tubes and tiny boxes…makeup? I got a mental image of putting on creams and powders to make my face soft to touch and beautiful for others to see. Weird. That seemed like something Princess Aquamarine would do. She loved to dress to impress when she wasn't pretending to be a dock worker.

On top of the desk, my fingers glossed over a peculiar flat and glassy box. An…iPhone. What the slanders was that? Yet, somehow, I knew not only what it was called, but that it had a name.

"Siri," I asked, "where am I?"

A pleasant woman spoke back, "You are on Ranch Road 33, in Big Spring, Texas. This location is labeled as 'Home.' The temperature is currently seventy-eight degrees outside."

Slanderous words, if this was a dream, my mind was more inventive than I thought.

Continuing around the room, I found a door. I retrieved my walking stick before emerging from my bedroom. My fingers trailed along the bumpy walls as if I'd done this several times before. My stick warned me of a familiar floor change as a giant rug carpeted a large room—the great room. I found a piece of furniture exactly where I expected it. It was a couch made of leather, yet the material was worn and softer than even my dad's throne of furs. My stick hit something harder; a wooden table kept within arm's reach of the couch for setting down drinks and other things my dad used.

The rug ended and the wooden floor continued bare into the kitchen. I circled the large marble island with the double sink and barstools. Moving into the breakfast nook, I continued through a door to the newer addition of the house. There was a mudroom hallway between the garage (a storage room large enough to keep two entire carriages!), a utility closet, and my dad's bedroom. I didn't need to enter the rooms to feel around and confirm this. The knowledge came naturally as if I'd done it before, like repeating a dream and knowing what would come next.

I returned to the great room to exit the house to the back porch. Little paw steps announced Rayban following me. The early evening sun warmed my skin, and I reached down to pet my dog.

Voices spoke and laughed in the distance. The cottages. Dad hired men to help with the cotton fields. The seasonal work was too short to set a housing contract, and anything available would require a commute. So, we provided on-site furnished housing for our temporary workers. By the sounds of it, they were enjoying the long day off from work. They sounded jovial, and my curiosity grew. I tapped my stick back and forth, stepping down the porch, into the grass, toward the voices. I took ten steps before realizing that I had nothing to lead me back to the homestead.

Turning around, there were no sounds or smells to guide me back. Only the sounds of a boisterous laugh from the temporary housing. Rayban whined beside me, but maybe one of the workers could lead me back.

Slightly more cautious, I walked toward the voices.

It sounded like two men, one particularly louder than the other. Why did their voices remind me of going home? Not of Ormio, but the feeling of peace all the same.

"To make a long story short," the loud voice said half with laughter, "the doctor told me to deal with the pain by resting, drugs, and Mariner Baseball. You know, nothing too exciting."

There was a low grunt that could have been a laugh, then a quiet question, "What is Mariner Baseball?"

The first man swore under his breath and muttered, "You're that new to America? Gall, this is going to be a long sum—what's that?" A little louder, slower, and more pronounced, he asked, "Did you see that? Something's outside."

"What is it?"

"Nevermind. Wait here. I'm going outside to check it out."

A door screeched open. I had to be close. Did he see me? Or was there someone or something else outside with me?

Some rustling caught my ears, but what direction did they come from?

Apparently, right in front of me.

My face collided with a boulder. I bounced back and landed on my rump. Rayban barked twice, and the boulder grunted.

"Hey," a loud masculine voice shouted. "Watch where you're going!"

I laughed, incredulous. "Are you serious? I'm blind! You watch yourself!"

"Oh," he said, immediately pacified. "Wow, you look…"

I had no idea how I looked, but his drifting tone seemed more complimentary. Still, I worried. "Is my hair a mess? Did I rip my clothes?" Slanders, I hoped I wasn't inappropriately dressed for a man's company.

"No, sorry," he said. "You look fine. No scratches or bruises from what I can tell. But you...wow, you look a lot like my fiancée."

I twisted my face in his direction to make sure I heard him right. Dot and I were often told how much we looked like each other, but I'd never resembled someone's fiancée. "In that case, are you the type of man to marry a woman based on her looks? Your answer will tell me whether or not to be offended."

He laughed, strong, hearty, and contagious. "Oh, it was a compliment. She's beautiful, but more than that. You could be her doppelgänger. Here." A rough hand wrapped around mine, catching me by surprise. The large hand yanked me up to my feet. I started to bend back to the floor to search for my walking stick when the large hand landed on my shoulder. I felt the smooth coldness of my stick rub against my arm.

"Thanks," I said, taking it.

"Sorry for knocking you over," he said. "My fiancée's deaf, and I'm hard of hearing, so I kind of know how being labeled as 'disabled' can suck. You're the farmer's daughter?"

"Ruby," I said, habitually dipping in a little curtsy. "Uhhh..."

My dream memories told me of a different—more common—greeting. Shuffling a little with awkwardness, I straightened and reached my hand forward for an introductory shake.

There was a light chuckle. Yep, my hand was probably nowhere near his direction. He stepped to the side then met my hand with his own. It was rough with callouses and entirely swallowed mine. It was also warm like the summer sun, yet dry and smooth from the cotton work. Swallowed and warm…like a wolf's stomach.

I shuddered and suppressed the fear. Trying to act normal, I asked, "Are you going to tell me your name?"

"So you can report me for throwing you around?"

I scoffed. "I could learn your name soon enough. I've heard your voice, felt your hands—I could pick you out if I had to."

"If there's no escaping it, my name's Leo."

"As long as you promise not to 'throw me around' again, I'll have nothing to report. It's been nice to meet you, Leo. Now, I could use an escort back to the house."

Chapter 5

RUBY

My dream continued with a rooster's call. I jolted from sleep and blinked, but saw only black. Right. I was stuck in this blind dream.

A wet nose bumped against my hand, accompanied by a little whimper.

"Hey, Rayban," I said, sliding my hand over his neck and back. Blind, yes. But also protected and loved by this fluffy animal. "Dog" was such a small word for something that took up so much space in a person's heart. "Come on. Let's go get some breakfast."

I barely needed my walking stick as I listened for Rayban's feet ahead of me, following his padded footsteps and recognizing the change from the wood flooring to the rug to lift my feet slightly higher over the rug's edge.

"You're up!" my dad's voice called from the kitchen. "I left some milk for you if you want cereal for breakfast. The guys have already started working, but I wanted to check on you. How are you feeling today?"

"Better," I said, sitting at the breakfast nook. Rayban sat next to my chair and rested his chin on my thigh. I imagined him looking up at me with adorable puppy-dog eyes, begging for a bite. I smiled and scratched him behind the ears.

My dad grunted with a hint of a laugh. "You look better. That's good. I gotta go, but I love you, okay? Don't spend all day listening to books and crocheting, alright?"

That sounded like a fantastic way to spend my day. Thanks for the idea.

He must have seen my expression as he added, "I'm serious, Biddy. The chickens need to be fed, dishes need to be done, and you need to practice the trumpet if you want to get those scholarships you talked about. If you slack off for the summer, you'll fall behind."

I groaned. "Fine." There were worse punishments for laziness. I was actually a little disappointed that he didn't ask me to join him in the fields. I could water and pull weeds. But that strange dream–intuition told me that they were doing more than watering the fields and pulling weeds. They worked with giant machines to plow, plant, disinfect, and harvest. It was Dad's job to farm. Without Mom, it was my job to care for the house.

So, I did just that. I fed the chickens, washed the dishes, and wiped the counters clean. Every little task was different without sight. I jammed my fingers more than twice while feeling around for dishes and where to put them. Though the work was more laborious than my usual chores, they seemed far more simple.

As a princess, my chores usually consisted of studying histories, practicing arithmetics, accounting, and writing. Every morning, my sisters and I went to the temple to write prayers for our people, distributing the extra food from our previous dinner. Then, at home, I organized food supplies for Dot to plan meals while Dia contacted the markets for any extra ingredients. As the youngest, Opal managed the floral sets and dinnerware.

I was left to do everything on my own in this dream, but found a surprising relief to realize that I only needed to care for my dad, me, and our six hired helpers in this home that was considerably smaller than Ormio's fortress.

Considering what to make for dinner, I lost myself in a list of recipes, fascinated by the concept of reading letters via little bumps then amazed by the spices included in the simplest of meals. Deciding to ease myself into my blind baking, I pulled out the flour for a plain loaf of bread.

I relied on raised lettering to know which ingredients and measuring tools to use. I needed to depend more on my other senses; smelling the yeast, feeling the water temperature on my wrist from the incredibly convenient indoor faucet, listening to the beep tones on the miraculous timer, and tasting the—hmm, this bread was going to be divine. Kneading the dough seemed more personal as I pushed and pulled, sprinkling water to make it just the right consistency.

While waiting for the dough to rise, I pulled out my trumpet. It was larger than the horn I played in Ormio, but—oh! It sounded beautiful! Clear tones echoed through the house without a rasp or squeak. I let my dream-instincts take over as I played a piece by muscle memory. Jazz? It was like nothing I'd ever heard before, nothing I could have imagined. I never knew a single tune could be so emotional.

Where was this coming from? Was this me?

I wished my siblings and friends could hear me as I played piece after piece, practicing even when my hands and mouth hurt, switching between melodies of this world and Ormio.

"Biddy!" Dad called from outside. "Did you want to join us for lunch?"

Oh, right. Food.

I hurried to put the doubled dough in the bread pan for its second rise, then went out to the porch where my dad prepared lunch on a grille while chatting with his workers.

I felt my way to the table where I smelled meat and toasted bread. The bread was like extra long rolls cut in half lengthwise, and the meat turned out to be smooth versions of sausages. Hot dogs? My dream-instincts told me that it went well with mustard and ketchup. Dad liked to add pickles and coleslaw—gross.

Following my dad's voice, I sat beside him and Rayban rested his chin on my leg.

Speaking around his food, my dad said, "I've never heard you play some of those songs before. When did you learn those?"

I shrugged. "A while ago."

"Thank you," a quiet voice said from the corner, "for the music. It was beautiful."

Another voice from across the patio scoffed. Leo? "You know 'beautiful,' but you don't know 'farm?'"

"Farm," the quiet voice repeated.

"Yes, we've established that. We're on a farm. Good job."

"Ah, give the kid a break, Leo," Dad chastised. "Shino's only been here for a week. All things considered, he's doing pretty good."

A few of the other workers joked and introduced themselves to me, but I had to admit my interest was focused on the two youngest workers that I'd run into the night before. I listened to their conversations, especially curious in the rare moments that Leo and Shino spoke. They were opposites in so many ways. One loud, one quiet. One assuming and bold while the other polite and reserved. One preferred country music while the other preferred classical and pop.

A couple of the other workers spoke quickly in a language I partially understood—Spanish?

I could listen to them talk all day, but their lunch hour ended all too soon. They returned to work in the fields, and I returned inside for the incredible temperature-controlled air. Dad hadn't given me more chores for the day, so I finished the bread and considered what else to make for dinner. I had a few hours to waste, so I grabbed my iPhone from my room then went to the rocking chair with my crochet projects.

The hand-held phone was a true marvel. I asked Siri to read a book to me, and it asked "Which one?" then gave me a seemingly never-ending list of titles. How could such a tiny thing contain so many stories? Unable to pick a favorite, I asked it to start with the first one.

Rayban laid next to me as my phone read to me about a young woman going to live in a magnificent city away from her country home. She met a handsome young man who had violent tendencies.

He was more wolf than man, but I hoped the heroine would tame his heart.

A couple of hours and many crocheted rows later, a timer reminded me to work on dinner. Reluctant to pause the story, I waited for the chapter to end. Of course, it ended on a cliffhanger, so I waited another few minutes before forcing myself to stop the reading.

Feeling my way back to the kitchen, I rummaged through the cabinets and storage for the supplies to make a beef stew. The smell of fresh bread tempted me while I baked, and I snuck a nibble or two between chopping ingredients.

The stew wasn't quite ready when Dad returned, groaning with sore muscles and sun-toasted skin. He helped me with the final steps of dinner preparations, then we sat to eat together. The dinner table felt empty without my mom, Dot's banter, Opal's chatter, Dia's scolding, and even Cephas's silence. Instead, Dad asked about my day, and I asked about his.

My ears were especially in tune whenever he spoke of the youngest two workers. He seemed pleased with Leo's enthusiasm and Shino's eagerness to learn, praising the energy of youthful workers.

"And if anybody asks," he said, "Shino's sixteen. He's technically your age, but fifteen's the legal working age in Japan, and his family couldn't afford for him to come to America any other way. Since he's only part-time, the lucky duck gets off after lunch. He says he spends his off time in his cottage, studying English and school stuff, but if he tries coming into the house, sic Rayban on him. He knows the rule; no employees in the main house."

I wasn't exactly sure what he meant by all of that, but a dream-instinct remembered Dad occasionally paying cash to "illegal aliens" who needed the work. "I don't care what the government calls them," he'd say, "they're human beings who need food and shelter, and they're willing to work for it too."

We enjoyed the evening with relaxing activities. I continued my crochet project while Dad turned on a speaker (TV?) that played various comedy skits. It was like the jester festival in our living room as comedians and hosts acted scenes with jokes. An unknown crowd laughed with us. Add more butter to the bread smell and the sound of my sisters jabbering beside me, and I could have been home.

When the dream continued the next morning, I was almost as content as I was sad. The cons of being blind and missing my siblings were still there, but I found new pros to add to the tasty foods and loving pet dog: instead of caring for a warring kingdom with thousands of people, all I needed to worry about was the people on this farm. Also, as much as I loved Dot, it was nice to do and have things without needing to share.

The next couple of days passed this way. I lazed about breakfast, did some housework, practiced my trumpet, joined Dad and the workers for lunch on the patio, then worked on a crochet project while listening to a book until it was time to prepare and eat dinner. Depending on Dad's mood, we'd either talk and play a brail version of Scrabble, or Dad would watch TV while I listened or continued reading and crocheting in my room.

On my fifth dream-day, Leo didn't join us for lunch. When I asked after him, Dad said, "He isn't feeling well. I'm guessing it's homesickness, but it's hard to know. Would you mind making a big pot of chicken noodle soup tonight for dinner? We can share it with Leo and the others."

"Sure," I said, reviewing what I remembered from the recipe...then mentally mapping where I could find the recipe.

Wanting to make the best batch of soup ever for the intriguing Leo, I set to work directly after lunch finished. The best thing to pair with chicken noodle soup was fresh rolls, and those needed time to rise. After preparing and separating two dozen rolls, I set them aside to rise and grabbed the materials needed for the soup. Making such a large batch required more time, not to mention the extra time I needed to carefully and blindly cut the ingredients, holding them down with the tips of my curled fingers, rocking the knife against the cutting board and my knuckles. I added a generous helping of spices until my nose became drunk on the smell.

Maybe I'd been a little too eager to make something delicious to share with Leo as I finished the soup with plenty of time to spare. I put the soup on a low simmer and waited to add the noodles that came in a bag, all hardened and pre-shaped. It was odd…and incredibly convenient.

As soon as the back door creaked open from Dad's return, I raised the temperature again and dumped the noodles into the soup.

"Wow," Dad said, "that smells amazing."

"Are you talking about the soup or the rolls?" I asked.

"Both. Did you make enough for us too?"

"There should be enough for everyone to have three rolls." One could never have too many rolls. Hoping not to sound too eager, I asked, "Can I deliver them?"

"Sure," Dad said. "You'll need to take the cart and roll it up the driveway to keep it from spilling. Do you want me to help?"

"No," I said. Yes, I sounded eager.

Dad chuckled with a hint of confusion in his voice. "Alright, but take Rayban with you."

I could agree to that. After taking a serving for himself, Dad helped me load the cart with the soup, rolls, utensils, and bowls for each of the workers. Pulling the cart behind me with Rayban as my guide, I rolled the cart down the paved walkway. It was a less direct route, but the cemented pathway let me roll the cart to the cottages without too much trouble. Even with the breaks every two steps, Ormio had never known such smooth pathways. After following the path for a good minute, I reached the three little houses in a row. Each tiny house was furnished with two beds, a small kitchen, a bathroom, and a little living space.

Of course, I only assumed this from my dream-intuition.

I stayed outside as I delivered the soup and rolls to the first two homes. Shino had temporarily moved into the middle house, afraid of catching Leo's sickness. That left the last one with Leo.

Leo groaned the moment before I opened the door. With the creaking of the door came sounds of a little yelp and rustle of fabric.

"Don't you knock?" he yelled.

"Why?" I asked. "What am I going to see?"

"Uhh," he slurred. "Right. Still, it's the principle of privacy. You shouldn't just barge in on people."

"I wasn't sure if you'd be fit to answer the door. I brought you some soup. Does that make it better?"

He grunted. The sound seemed half in annoyance, half in gratitude, but mostly as a relenting "fine."

I took a couple of careful steps toward him, less familiar with the layout in his cottage.

"Here, I can get it, just…how blind are you?"

I raised an eyebrow at him. "My vision is as clear as the inside of a wolf's stomach."

"Ew," he verbally cringed. "I'll take your word for what that's like."

His bed sheets rustled, and heavy footsteps approached me. Calloused fingers grazed mine as he lifted the bowl from my hands.

"Thanks," he said. "This smells amazing. Reminds me of home."

I smiled. "That was the point. What were you doing that required so much privacy?"

He grunted, his voice returning to the bed, and the frame creaked under his weight. "Reading an email."

"E-mail…" I said, slowly, picking apart the unfamiliar word. Was it a variation on male, chainmail, or mail like a letter? My dream-intuition said it was like a letter. That made sense if he was reading it.

"Oh, sorry," he said. "You still use an email, right? Just with text-to-speech? These days, it seems impossible to connect with businesses without one."

"Sure," I said. My dream memories said I had one. I should probably check that. "Who was your mail from?"

"My brother, Chase. He's in San Antonio for a summer exchange. My mom asked me to find a job in Texas to keep a closer eye on him, but Texas is so big, he's still four and a half hours away."

Four and a half hours of what? Walking? On horseback? No, intuition said it was in those weird carriages that rumbled with sound and vibrations down roads at unnatural speeds. Regardless of the mode of transportation, it was still a day trip.

Pretending I knew all of that from the start, I smirked. "You have a brother? Is he younger or older?"

"Younger. He's fifteen."

I wiggled my eyebrows. "My age? Tell me then, is he a lot like you? Is he handsome?"

Leo laughed uncomfortably. "He's trouble. He plays life by his own rules and doesn't like to stick in one place for long."

"Sounds like you," I said, grinning. I leaned against the wall, hoping to look as attractive as I felt. He could be studying me now, appreciating my appearance, stepping closer, and I wouldn't even know. My heartbeat quickened at the thought.

He chuckled to himself. "It's crazy. I left home to find work where my fiancée wouldn't distract me too much. But you look just like her. No matter how far I go, there will always be reminders."

He'd been studying me after all? Even if it was to compare me to his slanderous fiancée, my cheeks warmed.

"Dad says you have homesickness?"

Leo grunted. "I'll be pretty annoyed if that's all this is. I feel nauseous, but won't throw up. I'm tired, but I wake up with chills after dreams about stupid stuff."

"Dreams?" I asked.

He grunted softly. That wasn't an acceptable answer.

"Can I tell you something crazy?" I asked. I took his silence as a "yes," and said, "I think I'm dreaming."

"About what?" he asked.

"Everything. I'm not from here, yet even the strangest parts—like being blind and having a hand-held device read stories to me—all feel natural. It's like I've been doing this all my life."

"Haven't you?" he asked.

"No. I…" I paused, unsure how to say it without sounding crazy. Or was it too late for that? "I'm not from here, and only my dad followed me here. I don't know why he's here, but not my mom. I have an older sister and brother, a younger sister…and I have a twin sister."

My useless eyes burned and grew wet. Considering the many times and ways we fought, I hadn't expected to miss my siblings this much. Most of all, I missed my mom. I missed her calming presence and her willingness to help us, no matter our struggles.

"Dang," Leo said. "What happened to them?"

"I don't know," I said as the first tear fell. "I was supposed to warn them of the dangers coming…but I didn't make it."

"You were taken away?"

"I don't know!" I snapped, annoyed at my own emotions. Garnet came to Dot and me in Othium, asking for help. We went to collect Pearl, but the traitor, Tanzi, got to her first. Garnet didn't feel safe traveling on the main roads as we went to warn my family. Hungry and needing sleep, we came across a little cabin. We thought it was empty, but a little old woman returned home…The old woman—Tanzi?—no, the *wolf* had tricked us, and now I had no idea if my family was safe. I felt safe here with Dad. There was no war with Huiess. Instead, there was a peaceful quiet on the farm, and I had a lovable pet dog. Could I bring the rest of my family here?

Leo mumbled, "Sorry."

The couch squeaked as Leo adjusted his weight, then a couple of heavy footsteps brought him to me. He rested his tough hand on my shoulder, tapping it like he wasn't exactly sure how to comfort me. Then, his hand slid around to my back and pulled me into a bear hug. Yes, that was what I needed. I let my tears fall despite the comfort I felt in his arms.

He started to pull away, but I tightened my hold around him. Noticing my reluctance, he kept his arms around me until I eventually loosened my grip.

"Um, I hope you don't catch my sickness," he said.

"Homesickness isn't contagious," I murmured. "And somehow, this feels more like home than Ormio."

He grunted a little again, and cleared his throat. "Thanks for the soup and rolls. I'll try to get better soon."

I wiped away my tears and smiled back. "Please do. I missed you at the luncheons."

Chapter 6

EMER

By noon, Hanzo, Thachuma, and Jesse set off northward while the princes and princesses headed south-west. With Mica sharing his horse with Pearl (which she politely refused until seeing Emer and Caden share a saddle), they filled the carriage mostly with supplies. Hanzo happily abandoned his house in the forest glade, offering anything they needed, including discarded dresses from his departed mother. Emer had two new gowns from Jesse altering Charlotte's wardrobe, and Marin accepted the task of altering her other three gowns for her own purposes. Pearl happily accepted the donated clothes from Hanzo, finding them large, but less extravagant and more fitting to her own tastes. Without the time to appropriately alter the large dresses, Pearl pinched the skirts halfway, pinning them to her waist where she tied the loose fabric back with a sash.

Emer grinned at her younger sister. "You woke up yesterday and you already want to set fashion statements?"

Marin eyed Pearl's pinning with concern. "If you recall, Pearl's choice in clothing truly swayed the people's. Are you sure this is a good idea?"

Pearl laughed, spinning in her hand-me-down fixer-upper like a model. "If I truly wanted to influence the fashions, I would take a note or two from England's. Their fine fabrics were softer and more fluid than linen, yet stretched better than a loosely knitted blanket."

"Elastic," Caden said. "Don't ask me how it's made, but I know it's a stretchy material. These memories from another mind are truly boggling. What have you learned, Mica?"

His friend blinked and blushed as he glanced back at Pearl. "I played around a lot with an odd machine called a camera."

"Oh, yes!" Pearl said. "You taught me how to take photos! You showed me pictures of Emer—do you remember taking photos with Mica?"

Emer grinned. "Of course. I rarely saw his face from how often it was hiding behind that contraption."

Marin leaned into her husband's back. "I find it incredible how you two had similar experiences that were vastly different from mine. While you two went sight-seeing, I had to fight for my life against the sea in a boat I barely knew how to sail."

"That was some sailboat," Ranae said dreamily. "Imagine if we upgraded our own boats with those underwater mills called engines."

"I was most fascinated by their communication devices," Emer said, gesturing to her vine phone that coiled on the carriage.

Pearl perked at the sight. "You made a smart phone using your plant magic?"

"Not exactly," Emer said. "According to Caden, my vine phone is similar to an early prototype. Two carriers may be separated by two hundred meters and communicate with each other, though they must be connected."

"How fascinating," Pearl said. "Mica said that his camera worked primarily by manipulating light. I wonder if I may use my power to create a 'prototype' as you have."

Discussing the possible ways to imitate England's technology kept them more than preoccupied while they rode.

They pushed through the forest to reach the town of Denebrae by sunset. They entered through the main Shoreline Road, passing wild farmlands, empty residences, and vacated artisan shops. Similar to

Somnus and Lithus, most buildings stood precariously between newer pines and spruces.

As the main street took them by the docks, Ranae asked, "What happened to all the boats?"

Emer squinted through the mist and decayed warehouses to mentally repeat Ranae's question. Not a single rope tied to the docks. Some of the docks had collapsed into the water or had planks missing. Had they been sabotaged?

Looking ahead, however, dozens of chimneys smoked on the western and upper portion of the town.

"Life!" Mica cried, pointing at a pub on the road, opposite from the docks. Dim candle and firelight glowed in its windows as the lowering sun stretched cold shadows across its battered sign, "Brave Man's Pub." The pub was slightly less run-down than its neighbors, but likewise spotted with moss. The mist kept the feeble lights from flowing far.

Pearl worried her perfectly shaped eyebrows at the building. "Perhaps some company might cheer the place a bit."

"Er, Pearl," Marin said, "some people and places prefer to stay in the dark. I suggest we continue to the old Uptown. The majority of the population seems to have moved up the hill."

"Agreed," Caden said, urging his horse to hurry past the shadowed pub. One hundred harvests ago, Emer had known the main part of town to settle against the bottom of the western hill and branch along the docks. Some ill-kept buildings sported lights and chimney fires farther from the docks, but it seemed that most of the population had migrated to the clearer skies of the western hill. Indeed, as soon as they crested the switchbacks and reached the main Upper Road that traveled perpendicular to the coastline, they were greeted by a sight that Emer had almost forgotten.

Carts rolled down a maintained cobble street, pulled by laborers or mules. Buildings lined the road with various architecture to show off the different times they were built—lower levels made of stone and moss-spotted plaster, and newer upper levels were supported by wooden crossbeams. Candles lit the windows and balconies were lined with laundry. The town mostly consisted of humans, but there was a small group of dwarves and another of scaled folk— merpeople who took to the land. They bid good evening as they exited shops, but passed one another with downcasted indifference.

Emer had only a moment to smile at the sight of civilization before the citizens' faces turned to her group and turned into fear. Within seconds, the street emptied of pedestrians and drivers. People dodged into buildings, and carts were pulled into hidden alleyways. Doors shut, curtains dropped, and lights were snuffed.

"Wait!" Pearl cried. "Where did everyone go?"

Leo scoffed. "Figures."

Marin sighed. "We must be quite the sight. Several people riding into an old town—on horses and with a state coach, no less. Even a fringe town such as Denebrae can recognize a royal procession."

Caden frowned. "Usually, people come out to greet royal processions like parades. The only time I've seen them hide from one was when the ogres rode into the capital for the treaty."

"This," Emer said, "more than anything, shows what kind of kingdom Tanzi has created."

Pearl fumbled off of Mica's horse and cried to the darkened buildings. "We mean you no harm! Please, continue your tasks. We did not mean to disturb or halt your activities."

"Pearl." Mica dismounted to help her and frantically searched for a solution to Pearl's cries.

He bounded to the nearest door; a hair salon or fabric store based on the scissors sign. He gently knocked and pleaded with the hidden occupants, "Please come out. We didn't mean to scare you. Pearl only wants to see you smile, then she'll smile too."

"Mica," Caden moaned, "that's not going to work."

"All the same," Emer said, wiggling in her seat, "we should probably dismount. Walking beside our horses might make us appear less intimidating."

Caden agreed with a grunt, and ordered everyone to dismount. Leo walked his horse down the street, scoffing at the blackened buildings. "They acted like spiders, scurrying into corners, expecting us to stomp on them. Crying won't reach their ears. Perhaps the best way to reach them is to meet their expectations."

"Leo?" Caden asked, half in warning.

Leo paid him no heed as he marched up to a door with a post claiming, "Haven Inn." Leo pounded on the door.

"Open up, you disrespectful fools! We have foreign princes and princesses, and if you refuse to give us entry, we'll assume you're traitors to the crown and burn your building down!"

"Leo!" Pearl cried and stumbled on her dress as she hurried to him.

Shocked as she was at Leo's demands, Emer was half tempted to let him continue, curious what her little sister would try to do to stop the large hunter.

Before any more contention could rise, the door opened for Leo.

"Please," a male voice shook from inside, "we meant no offense to your highnesses."

Leo grinned back at Caden, pleased with his brutish success.

Emer stepped closer until she could see inside the opened door. The wooden inn was simple, with four round tables—three chairs each—and a bar with five high stools. What really set the inn apart from many others Emer had seen was the amount of seashells. Sand dollars spotted across the walls, large conches served as mugs, and the table candles sat in emptied clam shells.

The innkeeper was on his knees and bowed his head with reverence, but his whole body shook. He wore a long-sleeved shirt with no tunic and long trousers. He also wore a scarf tied around his neck, as if to hide the blue-purple scales on the sides of his neck and jaw. Pearl dashed past Leo to kneel beside the innkeeper and wrap her little arms around his shoulders.

"Thank you for welcoming us! Oh, is this your wife?" she asked, shifting to a woman behind the kneeling man. She took an involuntary step backward. "Please, do not fear us. How lovely, you have the most beautiful scales! Are they hereditary, or are you uniquely beautiful?"

"Stay away from her!" the kneeling man growled. He winced, as if immediately regretting his outburst, and ducked into a lower bow than before.

Pearl's shock turned into watery eyes. "Oh, please forgive me. Did I do something wrong?"

Leo guffawed. "You accidentally offend someone, and *you're* the one who cries?"

Yep, that was Pearl. Caden cleared his throat and stepped forward to explain, "The merpeople have been hunted for their scales. I'm actually surprised to see them living among humans."

Marin joined them in time to gasp with disgust. "That is horrible! Please, Mr. Keeper of the Haven Inn, we understand your protectiveness. Your wife is truly beautiful, though we say such compliments in earnest, not envy. Please, stand," she added, taking him by the elbows and raising him to his feet.

Ranae leaned against the doorway, remaining outside with Leo. "If your people are hunted, why do you live among the hunters?"

The innkeeper blinked and spoke slowly, obviously still unsure about the people surrounding him and what his place was among them. "The people of Denebrae spare us our lives in exchange for double payments and occasional beatings. With the curse upon Lake Imazhin, we had nowhere else to go."

"Beatings?" Marin's face twisted between pity for the merpeople and disgust at the prejudice. "Tanzi allows this horrid injustice?"

Ranae shook his head. "The war between Ormio and Huiess created similar problems, but Somnus was largely free of racial prejudices. Tanzi might rule the valley as a single kingdom, but it still seems broken."

"And cursed," Emer added with a nod toward the lake mists.

Caden retrieved his closest piece of parchment and charcoal. "Yes, we noticed the docks were abandoned and the mist still covers the lake. I thought it would be thinner here since its epicenter is the Queen's seat in Noz Isle."

"It is thinner," Emer said. "The mist went farther inland in Somnus and Lithus. With the cliff and distance from Noz Isle, the people were not forced to abandon Denebrae."

"True." Caden nodded and took a note.

"How exactly," Marin asked, "is Lake Imazhin cursed? They say that the mist makes one sleepy. Did this affect you under the water also? If so, then how are there still fish available to catch?"

The merman bared his teeth, hissed, and flared the fins behind his ears.

"Pardon me?" Marin asked.

The innkeeper's wife wrapped reassuring hands around her husband's arms. "Please, excuse my husband, but we do not speak of the curse on the lake or the…monsters that now inhabit it."

"Monsters?" Pearl squeaked. Mica rested a comforting arm around her shoulders, though his face seemed equally unnerved by the subject. Caden scribbled more earnestly with notes. He prodded and urged for more information, but the innkeeper and his wife remained tight-lipped, choosing to change the subject to matters of their room and boarding for the night. They split their group into pairs to take a total of four rooms, nearly filling the inn.

Noticing the discomfort of their hosts, Pearl asked, "Will you eat with us? Let us entertain you. Do you have any instruments?"

"We only have sea drums and a shell harp."

"Ooh!" Pearl clapped her hands with excitement. "May we perform for you?"

Leo shuffled uncomfortably and muttered, "By 'we,' you mean 'you,' right?"

At the same time, the innkeeper blinked at Pearl's request. "If you so wish it, Your Highness."

He left and returned with a set of metal bowls skewered by a pole and a lap harp with a large shell as its soundbox.

Emer gestured for him to pass the harp to her. Shell harps were tuned differently than the wooden harps she usually practiced—back when her father ruled—but after a couple of scales, she remembered the adjustments.

Marin had taken the sea drums, testing the tones of each bowl. "The tones are clearer underwater. Alas, we may make do. Ranae, do you remember the performance of the synchronized swimmers? They used mirrors to reflect the lights through the water."

"Truly a masterpiece." He nodded. "What will you play for us?"

"Here, Imazhin's Shores," Mica requested.

Caden frowned. "What song is that?"

At the same time, Pearl gasped. "You remembered?"

"Of course," Mica said. "I fell for you the first moment I heard you speak, but I didn't realize it until you sang that song."

Pearl's cheeks went as red as roses, while her face glowed.

The innkeeper yelped, taking a step away from Pearl's luminescence.

Pearl paid them no mind as she began to sing. Marin tapped the drums to add a tonal beat that rang through the inn. Emer plucked out the chords to add a harmony. A couple of other inn occupants—all merpeople—stepped from their rooms to watch.

After the final chorus, everyone clapped.

"Since when," a lone merman asked, "did humans learn to play sea instruments?"

Caden smirked. "A hundred years ago. Mermen and mermaids, may I present to you Emerald,

Aquamarine, and Pearl; the reawakened Princesses of Somnus!"

Chapter 7

EMER

Caden announced loudly to all occupants in the mermaid inn, "Here in Denebrae, you may soon hear news about the Midnight Forest being cured of its curse. We are here to tell you that it's true! The rumored Princess Pearl who slept therein has been cured from her poison with the help of her sisters, Princess Aquamarine—who lay in Lithus with her husband, the Navy Admiral—and Princess Emerald, who vanquished the thorny briars surrounding the Somnus castle."

Emer considered adding the names of Prince Mica Wright of Zubra, Prince Leo Bahr of Braeder, Prince Shinópu Chushiama of Chafan, and Prince Caden Seavers of Uldra, but the witnessing merpeople shrank back with every drop of a royal name. It was probably better for the former princes to stay anonymous for the time being.

"Please," Pearl said, "do not fear us. We wish for your companionship, in fact, we wish for your aid. I fear much has changed since we were poisoned. Too much has been lost. Too many have been hurt. We wish to end the suffering and injustices. We wish to rid Rezhina Valley of the poison that infected you as much as it did us."

Lowering herself to her knees, she pleaded, "Please, aid us in this cause."

"Please," Marin added. "We wish to restore the lake to its natural beauty. We wish to rid it of the monsters that forced you to abandon your underwater home. We wish to take away the cursed mist and sail its waters freely again. Please." She knelt beside Pearl. "Aid us in this cause."

"Please," Emer said, unwilling to let her sisters do all the work, "the ogres are at our doorstep, and our youngest sister, Queen Tanzanite, has done nothing to aid the northern grassland kingdoms. With Chafan, Zubra, and Braeder fallen, Uldra is on the brink. They need our help. If enough of us refuse to bow to tyranny, to instead stand against oppression, to fight the ogres and injustices of this land, we will once again be proud to claim this kingdom as our own. Somnus will not stand alone. We will wake Princesses Ruby and Peridot of Ormio. We will spread the word across the whole valley until you can reclaim the cities and livelihoods that were lost. We need to protect this land from the ogres and spread the word of our cause." Emer followed her sisters to the floor. "Please, aid us in this cause."

All was still and silent for too many heartbeats as Emer kept her face to the floor. Nervous, she stole a peek at their observers.

The innkeeper's wife was the first to step forward. She knelt before the kneeling princesses. "If you are who you say you are, we would be foolish to turn you away."

Her husband and other merpeople nodded or stepped forward. Relieved, the princesses stood.

Emer rejoined Caden's side and whispered, "This was why we needed Pearl."

He winked back. "You and Marin played a part too. Don't forget that."

The main hall of the little inn broke into several conversations. Pearl sang another song of praise while Marin asked the merpeople about their transition to land. Caden bounced between writing notes and explaining the northern ogre crisis as Emer supported him with her own ogre experience between supporting Pearl with harp accompaniment. Ranae and Leo gathered their own little crowd as they traded battle stories while Shinópu sat in a meditative pose and spoke only when requested.

The front door opened and closed several times as some occupants left, returning later with several more merpeople. A city policeman took interest in the gathering crowd, but soon enough, he joined the rally, waving in humans, dwarves, and even a troll.

Pearl sang more songs until supper was served—"For inn residents only." That encouraged most of the curious visitors to wander home, though some lingered. Caden barely touched his food for his parts in the conversations. Pearl, likewise, ate little between the song requests.

When Emer encouraged her to eat, she said, "Forgive me, but after multiple poisoned meals, I lack an appetite."

Caden remained at the table after supper, pushing his plate to the side to make room for his parchment. Knowing how he could become absorbed in his work, Emer removed his dishes. Tilting her head, she read over his notes.

"'Usually, people come out to greet royal processions like parades. The only time I've seen them hide from one was when the ogres rode into the capital for the treaty.' Princess Emerald's eyes glistened with tears like dew on grass in the sunrise. 'This,' she said, 'more than anything, shows what kind of kingdom Tanzi has created.' I dare say," Emer said, biting back her smile, "you make my eyes sound magical. I thought you wrote non-fiction."

"History is formed by the eyes of the witnesses," he said calmly, but the back of his neck burned red. "You disagree with my point of view?"

She smirked and took the seat next to him. "I think your point of view might be a little biased. Do you mean to write down everything, word for word?"

"As best as I can," Caden grunted. "Who knows which words will strike the hearts of my readers the most? I must record it all, but I need to do it while it's fresh. The worst kind of history is a false one."

Emer slid a paper aside to view the one beneath it. "This is no small task. Perhaps you need an aide—someone to help you remember the conversations, actions, and to provide a second point of view for fewer biases."

He grunted again. "Mica used to help me, but he's been a little more than slightly distracted lately. Also, his perspective might be more slanted against anyone who makes a certain young woman cry, even if it's by accident." Caden nodded toward the fireplace bench where Mica and Pearl sat closely, giggling over some joke.

Emer waited five whole seconds for Caden to ask her for help. When he didn't, she offered, "What about me? I could help you take notes and remember conversations."

He blinked at her. "You sure? You don't find this boring?"

She shrugged and glanced over his notes again. "I like the way you phrase things, but I might make a few adjustments. For a less-biased perspective, of course." She added a wink.

He chuckled. "I don't mind if my readers see you the same way I see you. You're brilliant, and I highly doubt that my little book will be the only proof when all is said and done."

"Your 'little' book?" She guffawed. "If this is what you call 'little,' I shrink to think of your larger manuscripts."

He grunted again, this time with a half shrug and chuckle. "So far, I have enough notes to create more than two volumes."

"And we still have many adventures ahead. I think we made enough of an impact here that we may leave on the morrow."

Caden spared a perusal around the room, nodding at the conversations centered on the princesses. "You're probably right. We're close enough to Ormio that we may reach the border in two days. But only if we're ready to leave right after breakfast both days. That means getting some sleep tonight."

His words implied a goodnight and goodbye, but he hadn't said the exact words. Emer took the excuse to linger. Instead of standing to leave, she shuffled closer until her arm brushed against his. She desired to rest her head on his shoulder, but dared not to do more in the public area.

Marin spotted them from across the room and finished a conversation with some merpeople to join them.

"Prince Seaver," she said, "all the merpeople seem convinced that Lake Imazhin is cursed. While I cannot deny the odd mists that permeate even the afternoons, the merpeople speak of monsters that drove them to the land. This deeply concerns me, though they refuse to speak more about it. Do you have any research on the matter?"

Caden shrugged and sorted through his notes. "People in your days believed in the Lake Imazhin Monster, right?"

Emer waved her hand as if stories were no more than a fly around her head. "It was a myth that only the superstitious believed."

Marin laughed and rolled her eyes. "Which included every sailor I ever met. One in five fishermen claimed to have seen it, though one in five fishermen also told 'big fish' tales."

Emer wrinkled her eyebrows, confused, and Marin explained, "What? You never heard the 'big fish' tales? When a fisherman catches a magnificent fish as big as a whale, though it escapes one way or another, conveniently leaving him without proof of his obvious lies?"

Emer laughed. "You spent far too much time on those docks."

Her older sister accepted the tease with a proud smile. "I have no regrets. Regardless, in every tale of the Lake Imazhin Monster, the creature was solitary and docile. Even after a hundred harvests, I highly doubt that gentle myth became this pod of monsters that terrorized the merpeople away from their homes."

Caden nodded thoughtfully. "We confirmed the curse of sleepy mists that cover the lake, but I didn't know about monsters driving out the merpeople—monsters too terrifying to discuss." He paused to hold Emer's hand beneath the table. "Then I think of you exploring the docks in Somnus, letting go of the rope and swimming in those waters." He met Emer's eyes with worry. "If there really are monsters down there, please, don't do that again."

Emer wasn't sure if she was supposed to be touched by his concern or irritated by his protectiveness. She gave him a small nod and a smile. Marin cleared her throat to remind them of her presence.

"Then," she said, "I suppose our route to Ormio will continue by land?"

Caden nodded. "Until we know more, I wouldn't dare to travel on the lake."

"Sorry, Marin," Emer said, knowing how much her sister loved the water and probably yearned to return to it.

Marin released a small dissatisfied sigh. "Very well." With a glance around the room, she added, "It seems that Ranae is ready to retire for bed. Thank you, Prince Seaver, for your insights. Good night, Emer. Remember, stay on the dance floor."

Emer's cheeks blushed red like cherries. When attending Noz Isle's midnight masquerades, Marin had lectured Emer, Pearl, and Tanzi about never going "someplace private" with a man, to never wander the grounds without another woman, but to stay visible and locatable always. In short, to "stay on the dance floor."

Marin left them with a short glance at Caden, between her motherly stare at Emer. Emer groaned with embarrassment.

Caden frowned. "What did she mean by—"

"Nothing."

"Oookay?" he slurred, smirking at her sudden shyness. "Then I'll add this conversation to my notes and wait for you to correct my narrative."

"That conversation was hardly noteworthy for historical records."

"It began as a discussion of the curses on Lake Imazhin. The thought processes that lead to discoveries can be as valuable as the discoveries themselves."

Emer rolled her eyes and laughed. "You are insatiable."

Caden grinned and slid his hand around hers. "Thank you for offering to help me with my record taking. I'm a bit overwhelmed on my own."

"Did you want me to go over your notes tonight to see if you missed anything?"

"Not tonight," he said. "Just rest tonight. We can worry about it tomorrow."

Another goodnight without actually saying the word. Emer stayed, wishing to tuck herself under his arm, to rest her head against him and enjoy his nearness a little longer.

"Pearl, spare yourself," Mica's voice urged from across the inn's public area. "I love your voice and would happily listen to you sing all night through, but if you did, you'd have no voice in the morning."

"One more!" a couple of the merpeople called. Pearl turned her big brown eyes on Mica to join their plea.

He laughed. "Please don't look at me like that. They've been saying 'one more' since supper. At this rate, it'll never end, and I need your voice to answer my questions about whatever happens in my crazy dreams tonight."

Pearl giggled, then turned to her audience. "Please forgive me, dear friends, but I am being advised to retire. Also, I do not wish to keep you from your other activities."

"Boo! Who let the boy speak?" one of the mermen teased.

"Uh-oh." Mica smirked. "Looks like I'm being heckled. Time to go."

"Oh, no," Pearl said, reaching for him. "Without so much as a goodnight?"

"Give her a kiss!" one of the mermen called. Suddenly, their whole audience was on their feet, cheering. Emer lost sight of her younger sister as merpeople hooted and hollered, craning their necks for a better look. The commotion morphed into laughter and teasing chatter. The crowd shifted and slowly dispersed, but Emer's sister and Caden's friend were nowhere in sight.

"Sooo," Caden slurred with his eyes also on the scene, "if we don't want a repeat of that, I should probably say goodnight like a proper nobleman."

"Probably." Emer blushed. She still wanted to prolong their time together.

Why was saying goodnight so hard? She would see him again in the morning. His hand continued to hold hers as if he was unwilling to let go until the exact moment she decided to pull away.

With a small smile, he raised her hand to his lips, kissing the back without breaking eye contact. He'd given her a similar kiss in England. Instead of pain surging from her finger, a pleasurable chill shivered up her spine.

"Goodnight, Princess Emerald," he whispered.

She bit back her smile and murmured, "Goodnight, Prince Caden."

Pearl was brushing her hair into a sleeping bun when Emer entered their shared inn room. Instead of a candle, small lights dotted the ceiling with patterns of the stars.

"Beautiful," Emer said, a little awed. "Do you mind if I make myself at home?"

Pearl blinked her wide eyes. "Not at all. How?"

Emer smiled and cracked open the bedroom window. "Dear vines, grow upward and join me in this room. Sneak in through this window and fill this wall with your beauty. Bloom with leaves and flowers until every board is laced by you."

The vines obeyed and stretched through the window, crawling across the entire wall until it became a lacework of stems, leaves, and flowers.

Pearl gasped. "How lovely! It almost feels like we are outside on the grandest adventure."

Emer smirked back. "Stick with Caden, and you may find yourself camping outside more than you ever wanted. Having a bed-framed mattress beneath me is a rare luxury these days."

Her younger sister shuffled into her bed and balled her covers under her chin. "I suppose I shall stick with Caden so long as he sticks with you. You two seem quite attached."

"I could say the same about you and Mica," Emer teased back.

Pearl raised her covers over her nose and blushing cheeks.

Emer smiled, though a persistent concern nudged her mind. This was her first moment alone with her younger sister, her first moment when she felt comfortable to ask, "Pearl, you said that you met Mica in England…but you never saw Caden?"

Her sister blinked and raised herself from her blankets. "I saw pictures of him," she said, "and you. Mica took pictures of you two together and showed them to me. You looked…in love."

Emer blushed as she struggled to keep the sadness from her voice. "Yes, I was in love. Do you know what happened to the Honorable Caden?"

Pearl pursed her lips, confused. "He is here, in the room two doors away with Mica."

Emer shook her head slowly. "This Caden was born and raised as a Prince of Uldra. I wonder what happened to the man who was born and raised as a lord's son in England."

Pearl shed her expression and sat beside her sister. "As the Honorable Mica said, you took him to Somnus with you. You both disappeared from Tintagel that day."

"You mean he is gone?" Emer asked, her heart on the verge of breaking.

"No," Pearl said, taking Emer's hands. "I mean that the honorables have become one with the princes. The way Caden looks at you is exactly the same. Princes Mica and Caden have every experience of England. Mica says he gains memories every time he dreams. Every morning, Prince Mica understands me more and more, and our relationship deepens."

Emer rubbed her eyes from the gathering moisture. Reflecting on her time with Caden in Somnus, she likewise recognized his developing knowledge.

"Of course," Emer scoffed. "Caden is the type of man to welcome someone else's lifetime of experiences."

Pearl giggled. "Mica has said that the new memories feel not like an infringement on his true memories, but an expansion. Since they exist separately, and he was a good man in both worlds, he feels blessed by the goddesses."

Emer smiled at her hands, reflecting on the two similar hand-kisses; one from England and one just minutes ago. Honorable Caden had followed her to Somnus and became one with Prince Caden. They were the same man.

Meanwhile, Pearl kicked her feet back and forth while smiling at her ceiling of stars.

Emer grinned and nudged her sister. "Look at you. Have you ever felt this way before?"

Pearl's rosy cheeks burned as light emanated around her.

"I assume that was a 'no.'"

"I—" she hesitated, "is this love?"

Emer raised an eyebrow. "Only you can answer that. Marin knows a bit more on the subject if you want to ask her. She and Ranae seem even closer than before."

Pearl bit back her puffy smile. Looking up with her big brown eyes through her thick black lashes, she asked, "Do you love Caden?"

Emer's breath hitched. "I do."

Pearl's smile went even thinner as her cheeks blossomed. "How wonderful! Maybe one day, I will be as sure as you are."

Chapter 8

DOT

The drive between Washington and Texas was a long one (even without that lump poking me in the bum or back). We left the mountains of wild green pines for carefully manicured hills of apple orchards and grape vines, then crossed stretch after stretch of yellow fields and hills…all without leaving the State of Washington. Slanders, this *state* was bigger than the whole Rezhina Valley. And with the help of the beastly carriage, we passed it all before stopping for lunch sandwiches at a park.

According to the map, we were at Spillway Park that overlooked the McNary Lock and Dam of the Columbia River. A small group of men fished from the edge while a family of four laid out a meal on a bench and table. The little piece of heaven beside the marvelous dam boggled my mind (especially when Mom shrugged like she'd seen bigger). What other wonders would we see during our trip?

My favorite moments were when I spotted wild birds along the road. They liked to perch on the wooden posts of wire fences or soar high above the fields. I spotted a few hawks, a flock of songbirds that flew together like a quick cloud, and a striking black-and-white crow that my mom called a magpie. What a curious name.

Then again, in Ormio near the southern canyon, we had a small hovering bird called a blue thief (named for its color and tendency to steal seeds from the man who discovered them).

Despite the blurring speed of our travels and the strangeness of the scenery, the road trip to Texas was similar to any carriage ride in Rezhina. I spent the time away drawing birds in my art pad (these eraser things were magical!). We snacked on food without utensils or dishes (dried mangos? Individual bags of crackers? My favorite was a collection of nuts with dried grapes and a delectable thing called chocolate). Then, we stopped every few hours to feed the monster-carriage and ourselves (once at a "fast-food" restaurant called Arby's with the most peculiar sandwiches of thinly sliced meat and tangy sauce).

With at least one hand on the steering wheel and her eyes on the road at almost all times, signing conversations with my mom were sparse and simplified. I asked Mom about how she drove the beastly vehicle, and she taught me with an odd mix of nerves and excitement about my permit. She asked if I wanted to try for a stretch of the road, but seemed relieved when I said no. Eventually, I fell asleep within my dream between the long stretches of fields.

When I woke up with great mountains on either side of me, I almost thought I was back in Ormio. No, the buildings between me and the mountains were far too large, and the road was crowded with those beastly carriages. The mountains tapered down again until they turned into red cliffs. If the colors weren't striking enough with the sun setting over them, they became great plateaus and statues of stacked boulders, tall as mountains yet standing straight and narrow like human beings. What words had created such structures? Were they once giants turned to stone?

I tried drawing them and the bat that I spotted fluttering overhead before we stopped at an inn (hotel?) in a place called Moab. I had never known such a fancy inn with its own pool for swimming. Mom asked if I'd packed my swimsuit, and my mind flashed to a tight-fitting outfit that left my arms and legs bare. I blushed at the thought and shook my head. Mom still wanted to soak in the hot tub after the long drive, letting me sit on the edge in my dress with my feet playing in the bubbles. How were there so many?

I didn't remember seeing so many bubbles, even during a merpeoples' choir concert.

We retired to our room, where I laid down and struggled to get comfortable. The irritating lump remained beneath me no matter where I positioned myself on the bed or which side I lay on. I eventually ignored the lump, fell asleep, and dreamed of home.

I was riding through a forest, weaving between fat trees and ducking under spiky branches. These weren't the trees of my homeland. This was the forest near Denebrae. The birds that scattered before us were types that carved their nests into trunks or built large nests of needles. I wished to fly ahead with the birds, to have their speed as I rode in a gallop.

Darkness chased us.

I almost wished it was merely a dream, where the circumstances could change into my own happily ever after. Unfortunately, this was more than a dream. It was a memory.

My two companions wore red and were princesses of Rezhina, but that was where their similarities ended. One was my twin sister, Ruby, sitting behind me on our horse. The older woman was Crown Princess Garnet Reo of Somnus on her own horse. She galloped with her black hair coming loose from its braid and she wore the worried expression of a caretaker (worried, but not frightened or nearly as terrified as I felt).

"Keep running," Garnet urged us and her horse. "It should stop…eventually."

"Has this happened before?" Ruby whined, daring a glance back at the shadows that swallowed all light behind us.

"Not exactly," Garnet said. "Emer grew thorns, and Marin grew a whirlpool."

I wanted to ask how someone "grew" a whirlpool, but my attention became diverted as I yanked my horse to the side, narrowly avoiding a thicket. Ruby grabbed the reins from behind me, correcting our horse to continue forward before the darkness of Pearl's curse reached us.

My memory shifted as I no longer galloped through the Denebrae Forest, and Ruby was no longer behind me. Instead, I ran through the Ormytha Forest with only Garnet. No, Ruby wasn't with us, and the thought made me sick.

A flock of blackbirds took flight ahead of our path. Opal called them a sign of bad luck. What had disturbed them? I prayed to the spirits that it was Ruby, only Ruby, though a dark instinct told me otherwise.

"Faster," I said, half to myself, half to Garnet.

Our temporary home from the previous night poked into view between the trees. It was a quaint cabin with a rocking chair on the porch, a little garden to the side, a basket of knitting projects near the fireplace, and dainty plating for one. The sweet, grandma-like woman had welcomed us. I hoped she was alright too.

Before my heart could feel relief at reaching our destination, a small detail kept it on edge. A nest lay discarded on the ground near the roof. Some bird had found the cabin quiet enough to spend days building its nest there. But something had recently disturbed it, abandoning its nest and two eggs. One had broken.

A shrill scream broke the air, piercing my heart and echoing in my mind.

Ruby!

We were too late.

I ran past the window to the door, then screeched to a halt at the vision inside. The old woman attacked Ruby with too much speed, too much youth, and too much evil laughter. Ruby ran to the bed, pulling on the quilted blankets for cover. The old woman leapt at Ruby and grabbed her neck with a claw-like grip.

I screamed as Ruby collapsed onto the bed.

My sister. My twin sister. Ruby.

Garnet yanked the cabin door open, dagger in hand. The old woman looked up, recognizing us. She threw something to the floor that shattered, causing smoke to rise around her. We coughed and backed away from the door until the air cleared. The old woman was gone, and Ruby…

Garnet went inside and beckoned me to follow. As if I could move, transfixed as I was. I could hardly breathe. For a moment, despite our physical differences, I had seen myself—not Ruby—drop like a rag doll onto the bed.

"Dot! Come in, we need to stick together!"

My paralysis took an extra second before letting me go. I dashed inside, dropping to my knees beside Garnet and my twin.

"Ruby, wake up," I said. "Why is she not waking?"

Garnet wrinkled her eyebrows in thought. "Dot, can you see the claw marks on her neck? Do they look infected?"

I found four punctures on the back of her neck with the same spacing as the old woman's fingers. I nodded to Garnet.

"Shrews," Garnet half-cursed. It was the closest I'd ever heard the future queen come to using profanity. She groaned and slid a frustrated hand down her face. As soon as her fingers lifted, however, she was calm and determined. "Lay her on her back and elevate her face."

Ruby. If I could help Ruby, I had to try.

I nodded and used the quilt to help roll my sister into a proper position. Garnet uncorked a potion from her sack and asked me to open Ruby's mouth. She poured the whole bottle down Ruby's throat.

"What is that?" I asked.

"It will slow the poison," Garnet said. "We need to take her back to Oth—"

Wolves cried in the distance. I shivered as their howls grew into a choir, louder and closer.

"The curse is coming! Hurry!" Garnet grabbed Ruby beneath her arms and heaved. I grabbed my sister's legs and helped drag her to the cabin door.

A pack of a dozen gray wolves charged at us. They didn't bark, but bared their teeth and growled. Garnet set Ruby down to pick up a pan, waving it back and forth at the animals. More wolves joined the edge of the clearing. As if the first pack wasn't large enough, they were quickly joined by another pack, then another. What were they doing there? Could we escape them all?

They lunged for us, and my senses became lost between the weight of fur, the cry of growls, and scenes of the wild. They forced me away from Ruby. I cried out her name as she was pulled away from me. I waited for the pain, the biting, the clawing. It never came. I almost wished for the physical pain to distract me from the pain in my heart as they tore me from my twin.

The wolves discarded me at the edge of the clearing. Ruby was no longer at the cabin door. Was that her red cloak draped across the bed? I tried to step closer to see better. Any attempts to return to the cabin were met with ferocious growls.

Garnet stood beside me and slowly backed away.

"Have you ever seen so many wolves in one place?" she asked.

"No," I said. "It's unnatural."

Garnet gave a little gasp. "Of course! Thorns, whirlpool, darkness, and now wolves. They are not curses, but protection!"

"What?" I asked, more confused than ever.

"Come." Garnet grabbed my arm to pull me away. "Ruby will be safe. It is our lives that are now in peril."

We ran away from the cabin as yet another pack of wolves ran to join the crowd. I cried, worried about leaving Ruby behind, but they stayed outside. Wild dogs surrounded the cabin, almost like guards. I prayed to the spirits that they would protect Ruby instead of hurt her more.

My dream drifted to another memory, days later, as my horse galloped beside Garnet's. After running in terror, we finally made it to Othium. Our travels had been quiet as my mind continually replayed the scene of the disguised grandma grabbing Ruby with her claws. I kept hearing my sister's scream over and over and over.

We slowed only when we reached the city's gate. Garnet suggested we raise our hoods and give the guards false names as we entered. Were we in so much danger that we needed to hide ourselves?

Once inside, she asked, "Is there a place we can stay the night? It needs to be some place that you trust to keep us safe."

There was an inn who liked to give special treatment to their guests. My family visited them before, and they proved themselves to be loyal to the crown. Instead of saying all this to Garnet, I nodded mutely. I feared that if I opened my mouth, I would scream as Ruby had.

"Excellent. Lead the way, Dot."

Near the edge of the town, the inn was exactly as I remembered, except for the new maid who set up my bedding. Her hair was gray with a few lingering black stripes (or was it blonde with black stripes?), and she wore a necklace of vibrant red peas with black tips. Rosary peas? Though beautiful, I was fairly certain those were fatally poisonous if ingested. The old woman bowed and bid me a good night before shuffling to Garnet's room.

Garnet came in a moment later to ensure my comforts, wiping her hands with unease against her traveling dress in the same manner as her mom.

"I have a bad feeling about this place," she said. "Are you sure that we will be safe here? They seemed to go out of their way to make you comfortable." She nodded at my bedding.

The bottom five mattresses made a firm base of straw, then the next three were stuffed with wool, topped with another two of cotton, then another one of feathers. The very top mattress was a thick layer of woven blankets in case any of the feathers poked free from below. The pile altogether required a stepping stool to climb atop.

I settled in, but found myself rolling and adjusting positions.

"There's a lump in the bed," I muttered.

Garnet yawned behind her hand. "Can you kick it out or sleep around it?"

I twisted and angled myself, but couldn't ignore the lump from below. I kicked my heel on the lump to flatten it, then heard a small crack.

Like breaking a vial, the crushed lump seeped into the beds beneath me. A bitter aroma filled my nostrils, and I found my eyelids droop. I collapsed on the bed despite the persistent lump.

Somewhere in my drift toward sleep, Garnet shouted my name, and a raven cawed.

I woke in the Moab hotel, disoriented with that high pitch—no, Ruby's scream—still ringing in my ears. Would I gain my hearing again if I found a way to save her? First, I needed to wake up from this expansive dream, and some inclination told me that finding Leo was the first step to waking. I had to see him. An unknown desire grew within me, needing to know who he was, what he meant to me, and how he might help me return to Ormio.

As we checked out of the hotel room, I found a beautiful songbird. It had a yellow body with a red face and a yellow spot on its black wings. I studied it, hoping to draw it later.

How I wished to hear it sing. I asked Mom about it, and she angled her ears toward the bird. After a long moment, she pinched her fingers like a bird's mouth, bouncing it up and down to show the songbird's speed and pitch for its little chirp. Cute.

The second day of driving somehow felt longer than the first, even though it was technically shorter. Maybe it was the lack of changing scenery. Mom kept herself awake by blasting music with a bass that vibrated through my seat. I was entertained by watching her sing along as she sometimes added signs to her dance moves.

Apparently, her attention to driving drifted enough to catch the attention of a highwayman. Red and blue lights flashed behind us, bleeding into my mom's cheeks as she stopped the car on the side of the road. The highwayman came right up to my window as my mom rummaged through her purse. How much would he make us pay? Why had he stopped us among all the others on the road? Did he have a band of thieves stopping the others farther down?

He spoke to my mom, and she handed him a single card and piece of paper. Her driver's license? I had one of those, didn't I? Or a permit?

Despite the highwayman's clean clothing and my dream's intuition saying this was a different kind of highwayman (policeman?), I shied away from him in my seat, leaning hard on the ever-present lump beneath me. I asked my mom what was happening, and she signed back, "It's OK. I guess I missed the speed-limit change."

The policeman tilted his head at Mom. Moving with slow and stuttering gestures, he signed, "You know ASL?"

Mom pointed at me, spoke, and signed, "My daughter's deaf."

He nodded and handed back her papers, speaking words too mumbled for me to lipread. My mom smiled with relief and thanks as he waved farewell to both of us.

"What happened?" I asked.

"Apparently," my mom signed, "he thanked me for not pretending to be deaf as a way to get out of the ticket. He learned basic sign language after one too many people tried that."

Huh. I never would have thought of that, but I'd already learned how easy it was to brush people away simply because I couldn't hear them.

In comparison, the rest of the drive was uneventful. We arrived in Big Spring, Texas, in time for a late dinner at a Mexican restaurant, then stayed the night at another hotel. Mom said Leo's workplace was still a half hour away, but there weren't any closer hotels.

I woke early from more restless dreams of memories then was too anxious to return to sleep. After two long days in the car, I would see Leo.

Washing away my stench of the road trip, I dressed in my most flattering springtime dress. It was simple yet complex at the same time. While it required a shortened cloak to fully cover my arms (dream memories called it a cardigan), the dress was a single layer that draped loosely to my ankles. A long strip made of the same dress fabric worked as a belt around my waist. Never in Ormio had I ever seen such intricate patterns of pink flowers and little yellow birds overlaying twirling vines and leaves.

Too eager to wait, I jostled my mom awake, urging her to go. She slowly woke and dressed herself with little enthusiasm, then debated about grabbing food before heading over. The mention of food twisted my stomach, but was that with hunger or nausea? I argued to skip breakfast. Mom raised a skeptical eyebrow and signed, "Your stomach growled."

Fine.

The breakfast menu was almost expired by the time we found a restaurant (a diner?). The entire building smelled of butter and fried meats. I ordered pancakes, surprised by the amount of sugar and butter in the fluffy patties. Then it was topped with more butter, strawberries and bananas, and came with a separate cup of syrup.

I'd never been one to shy away from sweets before, but this dream's food was too sugary for my tastes.

Mom eyed me with concern when I didn't finish my food, but I excused my appetite with my excitement to see Leo.

Boxing away half of my meal, we returned to the beastly vehicle for our final leg.

The vehicle jostled me over pocketed roads (shuffling the lump under me from one side to the other). Blinking at the flat fields on either side of us, I asked my mom, "Where are we?"

Keeping one hand on the wheel, she signed back, "Almost there."

Really? Finally. How would he react to seeing me? How would I react to his reaction? What would he expect of me?

I wasn't sure what I expected either. Would I fall in love with him as deeply as my memories said I was? Or would we be stuck in an awkward engagement where I felt only kindness for him? If the latter, I hoped he helped me to wake as quickly as possible.

At the very least, I didn't want to make any conclusions immediately. If the drive took us two days, I hoped to spend at least four days in the area before driving back. Preferably longer, but with no indication of how we would be welcomed, I kept my plans limited.

Mom checked her phone map, the road, her map, then the road again. With quick one-handed signs, she said, "I think this is it."

I pressed my face against the window to spot the house partially hidden by a couple of large trees that stuck out amid the flat fields. Mom decreased our speed drastically as we pulled away from the main road and onto a long dirt stretch to the house. Approaching slowly, I studied the white wooden house with white columns and an aged white fence surrounding its front area (so much white). It had several tall windows with blue shutters (what was the point of those when they were always left open and the insides were covered with more slats?) and beautiful brick stairs leading into its fenced porch and up to its elegantly carved double wooden doors (did my mom appreciate the design too?).

The rumble of the vehicle stopped, but after going so fast for so long, I still felt like I was moving. My legs wobbled a little to stand on solid ground again. That slanderous lump continued to irritate whichever foot held the most weight.

I loved my mom, but she didn't understand my attachment to Leo. Honestly, neither did I. Not yet, but I wanted my time with Leo to be alone.

Before my mom could unbuckle, I asked, "Stay here, please?"

She frowned at me with irritation, but signed, "Thirty minutes."

Chapter 9

DOT

Leaving my mom in the car, I grabbed my art pad and flipped through my bird drawings to a blank page. Most people didn't know sign language, but most people in this dream land could read and write.

Scribbling a note, I marched up the porch steps and knocked on the door.

I held up a piece of paper with my handwritten introduction and waited. "My name is Dot. I am deaf. Is Leo here?"

Maybe the wait was only five seconds, but it felt unbearably long when unable to listen for footsteps coming. Was there a slight vibration in the ground from heavy feet?

A middle-aged man opened the door, wearing a red striped (plaid?) shirt with rolled-up sleeves and blue trousers that I came to know as "jeans." More shocking, I recognized the man as Dad, King of Ormio.

I nearly dropped my jaw and art pad. What was he doing here? I nearly ran inside and embraced him, but he stepped back.

He stared at me, completely bewildered. His mouth moved and ended on an "O" shape as he read my sign. He spoke again, but the communication I understood was the widening of the door and his hand gestures for me to come inside.

I stepped into the home with wood flooring and solid tan walls. My left view was blocked by one of those walls, "decorated" with a wooden cabinet, cluttered with items (probably tossed there after returning home). To my right was a dining area with a round table and four chairs. Instead of placemats and silverware, there was a deck of cards and stacks of tokens on top (poker chips?). Maybe it was less of a dining room and more of a games room.

The man who looked like Dad continued to stare at me with an unsure expression (he didn't know me?) as he continued talking, searching around the wall that blocked my view, his lips moving far too quickly. Based on the angle of his face and the wideness of his mouth, I guessed he shouted at someone unseen.

He studied me and held up his index finger, saying "One—moment? minute?"

A girl stepped into view from around the wall. She wore a white flowing shirt that tucked into the front of her bejeweled jeans. She wore heavy boots, but walked with shuffling feet. What surprised me the most was her face.

"Ruby!" I tried to shout. I probably just shouted, "Oo-ee!"

The girl who looked exactly like my twin sister jerked her closed eyes toward me as her foot nearly stumbled. Her mouth moved and Dad—her dad—answered. His eyes bounced between us, probably playing "spot the difference" as people liked to do with identical twins.

Ruby reached her hand forward as she kept her other hand on the shoulders of a medium-sized dog. The fluffy black pooch had a white neck and paws and a stripe down the middle of its face. What was it doing indoors? Then again, it wouldn't be the first time Ruby brought a dog inside.

Her dad took her hand then gestured for me to offer my own.

Slanders! She was blind!

I offered my hand, and the dad brought us together. (He'd give himself a headache if his eyes kept bouncing between us) Ruby's hand grabbed my own. I started to sign, "R-U-B-Y?" but her hand slid away from my fingers, up my wrists. Her mouth moved as her hand glided up my arm, shoulders, and to my chin.

Her eyebrows constricted with focus as her fingers reached my mouth. I mouthed, "Ruby?" There was no point trying to voice it, but Ruby's face became more confused.

Her face tilted toward her dad. Oh, he was speaking again. Ruby nodded.

The dad stepped before me. He patted my twin's shoulder and mouthed slowly with emphasis. "Biddy." (At least, I was fairly certain he hadn't said "pity" even though it looked the same.) Was Biddy her name? Then she wasn't Ruby?

I didn't have time to guess while the dad pointed to himself and continued talking, slowly. He still looked baffled by my appearance. The surprise was mutual.

"I. Will. Ed? Leo."

Leo! Thank the Words, his name was easy to lipread. It may have played a small part in my reason for initially befriending him. I smiled, and the dad seemed relieved that his message was received. He opened the door and jogged outside.

Biddy let the dog lead her to the door where she picked up a red-tipped walking stick. Then she followed outside.

Was I meant to follow? Slanders, I was following a blind girl into the fields?

Biddy walked out and down the porch steps naturally, then rounded to the left. The house property continued for several more paces until green fields of ten-centimeter cotton plants finished the horizon. Biddy's lips formed Leo's name before the dog dashed into the field, tail spinning and quickly out-pacing my dad look-alike. I followed the dog with my eyes over the field, finding a group of men working a large machine. They were smaller than my outstretched thumb, but somehow, I knew which one was Leo even before Biddy's dog reached him. He looked our way. Did he recognize me too?

The girl who could have been my twin's twin tilted her head as she listened for a shouted reply. Her face brightened with a smile that twisted my heart. It was the same smile that I found on my face whenever I thought of Leo. My Leo. Not hers.

Of course, if this girl really was Ruby, it would only make sense. Ruby always went after the same things I wanted. If I started horseback riding, she would too. If I wanted to go swimming in the lake, she did too. If I danced with an attractive man at the masquerade, Ruby always took the next one from him. While I enjoyed doing things with my sister, some things weren't meant to be shared.

I watched the girl as she ambled in front of me, swaying her stick in front of herself. All I needed was confirmation.

She angled her face back to me, speaking slow, but indistinguishable words.

There it was: the three moles under her ear that made a perfect triangle. It was Ruby!

I tapped her shoulder to make her stop walking. She did, and tilted her head toward me, listening. Did she forget that I was deaf?

I took her hand like she had taken mine earlier and slid it up to her neck. With my thumb, index, and middle fingers, I pressed against the moles.

She frowned at me, but I grabbed her index finger and pressed it to my neck, below my right ear, where I had a singular mole. Other than her redder hair and my greener eyes, the moles were another distinguishing feature between us.

Ruby's face opened with recognition. Her mouth moved, and I lip-read, "Dot?"

I pulled my twin sister into a hug. Her cheek and chest vibrated from talking. I rolled my eyes, pulled away, and gave my sister a tap on her cheek. "I cannot hear you!" I shouted, probably sounding like "Ai-annaw eeoo."

Ruby's face twitched into expressions easy enough for me to read her next words. "Oh. Right. Words."

I laughed and signed, "I know, right!?" As if she could see my signs.

Her mouth moved again, and she waved her hands around with frustrated motions that didn't translate into ASL. I tried to prod her toward the field again. If we could find Leo, he could interpret for us. If only I could explain that to Ruby.

Eventually, my sister's rantings shifted as her head jerked toward the field. A second later, the shepherd dog returned. It ran to Ruby's side, sat, then nosed her hand as if searching for a treat. Ruby crouched to pet the dog and rewarded it with words spoken from a pursed smile.

Leo was close enough that I pinpointed the moment he recognized me as his smile lit up. His eyes, however, were confused.

Still jogging across the field, he spoke and signed at the same time. "Dot! Why are you here?"

I signed back. "To see you."

And—oh, he was a sight to behold. He was a giant of a man, close to two meters tall and a muscled figure. His squarish face was emphasized by his short boxed beard and brown hair twisted into a top-knot. He wore the customary jeans and a red shirt (I recognized the T-shirt this time!) with a depiction of a wildcat created from white letters W, S, and U.

Slanders, he was even more beautiful in person. He was just as my false memories remembered, but better because he was real. Or at least, real in this dream.

He didn't stop jogging until his arms wrapped around me, lifting me from the ground, and swinging me in a circle. Slanders, he was strong too! I had no idea how to act in this stranger's arms. I felt like an amnesiac standing in a stupor while he acted like he knew me—no, *loved* me.

When he set me down, my hands stuttered through a series of unfinished questions. His eyes bounced back and forth between Ruby and me. Her mouth was moving. Apparently, both of us were talking to him at the same time.

He made a "T" with his arms as his mouth formed the verbal translation, "Time out."

Ruby stopped and waited. Leo continued to glance between us, imitating my dad look-alike.

Signing and speaking, he said, "Wow. I *wasn't* crazy. You two look very similar."

Ruby grinned and her shoulders shook with a chuckle. I smiled and signed while she spoke. "We're twins."

Leo frowned. "Sisters?" he asked and signed. "How? Switched at birth?"

Ruby's mouth moved quickly with unsure expressions. At the same time, I signed the general story about dreaming, and Ruby being my sister in reality.

"Stop, stop. Hold on." Leo raised his palms to stop us. His hands and mouth stuttered before he gestured, "What?"

Ruby reached for me. I grabbed her hand to help her to rest it on my shoulder.

Leo looked just as confused as ever. Welcome to the party.

"Did you two collaborate?" he asked with his hands and lips. "Is this a joke you two put together?"

"No," I signed. "She's my sister. Not here, but in O-R-M-I-O: my home. Our home." I finished, emphasizing the connection between Ruby and me.

Leo frowned deeper. "Where [unknown sign] O-R-M-I-O? What happened?"

"I don't know," I signed. "I'm still figuring it out. Ruby and I need to talk. Will you translate?"

Ruby continued to talk about something. Leo's eyes bounced again until settling on me. "Okay, she also says you're from that other place, O-R-M-I-O. You're…sleeping and dreaming…Here and now? In that place, she can see, and you can hear. You have the same mom and dad. You're…princesses? Okay, that's [unknown sign]." He pouted like he shared a joke and he just realized it was about him.

"No, no!" I signed. "It's true! Please, my sister and I need to talk. Please translate for us?"

Leo leaned back and gave me a downward stare, aghast. He frowned like he wasn't sure who I was. I cringed to think he was right. Then, he signed, "OK?"

I turned back to my sister and signed for Leo to speak aloud.

"You know we're dreaming? What do you remember last?"

Ruby's mouth moved quickly with eagerness. Leo lagged as he translated into sign language, but at least we were communicating.

"The last thing I remember," she said through Leo, "was being eaten by a wolf, but that had to be a dream, right? I'm dreaming now, blind in this marvelous world, so I can't be dead, right?"

"Eaten by a wolf?" I gulped. Had the pack of wolves eaten her after chasing Garnet and me away? "Slanders, I hope not. But, Ruby, do you remember what happened? Garnet and I saw the old woman attack you, and realized she was Tanzi in disguise. Garnet administered her sleeping drought to you, saying you were poisoned and sleeping like her sisters."

"Then, is this the afterlife, or are we dreaming? How did you come here? Did you die too?"

Leo interrupted our conversation with his own commentary. "What the [unknown sign]? Are you two reincarnated, or something? I'm not dead, so I can confidently say this isn't the afterlife."

Answering both Leo and Ruby, I signed, "We're dreaming. Probably. But how do we wake up?" I glanced at Leo, hoping he had the answer. I'd been sure of it, but how could he if he didn't even know we were asleep?

"I don't know," Ruby said through Leo. "Was I really attacked by Tanzi? I only remember being eaten by a wolf. That's why I see only the darkness of a wolf's stomach."

"That's awful." I grimaced. "If it makes you feel better, I only hear your screams from the moment you fell."

Ruby cringed. "You know, I think I prefer being blind, so yes, that helped."

"We need to find a way to wake up and get back home. You weren't eaten, simply poisoned through puncture wounds. Garnet and I planned to take you with us, but dozens of wolves came and surrounded you. I cried all the way back to Othium, but Garnet said you'd be safe."

"From what? For how long?"

"I don't know. All the more reason to wake up. Garnet wanted us to help convince everyone at Veriae to stay together, to find an antidote and not to believe Tanzi's lies. But…I never made it out of Othium."

"What happened to you?" Ruby asked.

"I don't know," I signed. The last thing I remembered was Garnet telling me to get some rest—that she'd stay awake and keep watch. (She looked like she hadn't slept in days.) I remembered trying to fall asleep, feeling bothered by a lump in the bed. Kicking at the lump had released something like a toxin that put me to sleep. I still felt the lump as a pebble in my shoe.

On the subject of reasons for my discomfort… there was the very large, very handsome, very confused, and very complicated man standing between my twin and me. We could discuss our memories later, though his presence was very present.

"Leo," I signed, "Ruby and I need to wake up. Can you help us?"

The large man shuffled with a quick glance at Ruby.

"I have no idea what's happening," he signed. "Can we talk, just you and me?"

Blushing and unsure, I nodded, and he explained to Ruby. She quirked an eyebrow and mouth corner to sass back. The interaction surprised me. Ruby only showed her sassy side to family and close friends. How personal was she with Leo?

A small flicker of annoyance sparked in my chest. Of course, she liked Leo. There wasn't anything unlikeable about him, and Ruby always wanted whatever I had (unless it related to bird watching. That was the only activity that I could truly call my own). Everything else I'd had to share with my twin sister, from clothes to men.

No, I wasn't going to share Leo. We were engaged, and (even if I didn't know the full extent of our relationship) marriage wasn't a three-horse hitch.

Annoyed and frustrated, I gave my blind sister a little push and said, "Go!" It probably sounded more like a tuneless moan, but the meaning couldn't be mistaken.

Leo stared in surprise at my action, and I huffed. "What—as if you never pushed your siblings?"

Frowning, Ruby called for her dog again and let it guide her back to the house.

Now that Leo stood in front of me, I was unsure what to say. Shuffling a little, I asked, "How are you?"

He balked back. "How am I? I'm working day to day, then you show up and say you're twins with my boss's daughter, and you're both possibly dead princesses from an alternate reality. How am I?" he repeated with an exasperated face. "I'm confused like an upside-down bat!" (Did that make him right side up?)

I couldn't blame him. With a sheepish shrug, I signed, "Same."

"How?" he asked with exaggerated gestures to express his frustration. "I wanted to see you again, but not like this. What's going on?"

"Sorry," I signed. "If I knew, I'd tell you. All I know is I'm dreaming, but this all feels real. Ruby said things I didn't know—things I can't make up. I have memories that don't make sense. Memories of you."

"What do you mean?" he asked. When I hesitated to answer, he held his palm up to interrupt my attempts to explain. "Nevermind. If you drove all the way to Texas to break up with me, don't tell me now. Please."

I hesitated again, and I might as well have told him we were breaking up. His face and shoulders sagged.

"That's not why I came," I signed and shook my head. "I wanted to see you. I hoped you would help me…and I missed you."

Like a lake wave, his shoulders and expression rose again. "I also missed you."

I smiled. "I'm glad to see you. We'll talk more after work?"

Leo nodded his fist eagerly. Then, he leaned toward me, pursing his lips. What was he doing—Slanders!

The moment he closed his eyes, my mind panicked, and my body stepped back.

He stumbled a little when he met empty air. Blinking, he signed, "What?"

Heart pounding like a runner's feet, I simply stared. It didn't matter if I had memories of kissing him (of his arms around me and his mouth against mine), he was still a stranger to me.

I took another step back, pinched my lips back, and signed back, "Sorry. See you later."

Then I turned and ran toward the house. Each step landed harshly on that phantom pebble under my foot. It hurt like slanders, but I couldn't stop, I couldn't look back. I couldn't stand even the thought of Leo's confused and heartbroken expression.

Halfway to the house, I tried to balance myself to land less on the pebble. Foolish attempt. The lump moved according to my weight. Instead, I landed directly on it.

I over-corrected my balance, twisting my ankle and losing the strength to hold myself upright. I fell to the ground with a scream to rival the one in my head as pain bit through my leg.

Chapter 10

RUBY

Jealousy was a well-known companion who frequently met me through my twin sister. I was no stranger to the hardening stomach, burning chest, and difficult breathing. Every activity I began with Dot started that way. Somehow, she always picked the thing I wanted most, then took it for herself. It annoyed me beyond words that she found a way to do it even in my dreams.

Leo's fiancée was my sister. She hadn't even been around, but she found a way to take him away from me too.

Yes, I was all too familiar with jealousy. Anger, however, was new. My jaw hurt from clenching my teeth.

My blindness had turned her simple push into a surprise attack. My stumble for balance made me want to punch her in retaliation. I wanted to call her Dodo and demean her worth in front of Leo then laugh like a hideous villain.

Why did she always get the things I wanted? What did she do to deserve Leo more than I did? What did she have that I didn't? Was it her greener eyes? A scary part of me wished to pluck them out and make her as blind as me.

Leo had said they grew up together. But that was a lie. She grew up with me and couldn't have known Leo any longer than I had. But if time was the only difference between his feelings for her and me, I could fix that.

I began plotting ways to keep them separate, reasons to keep Dodo away from him. If she wanted to wake up and leave this dream, then fine by me. I'd stay and keep Leo for myself.

It had irritated me to no end when he asked me to leave them alone to "talk." They spoke silently with their hands. I couldn't possibly eavesdrop on them even if I wanted to—and oh, how I wanted to. I wanted to linger to catch any whispers from Leo and make sure he didn't forget about me.

No, I would make him forget about Dodo instead.

Lucky for me, I didn't need to plot hard.

Rayban had barely led me to the back porch when I heard a tuneless scream. What a horrid sound.

"Rayban," I said, "get help!"

He barked twice and dashed to the fields. I grabbed hold of the porch railing and waited. Shameless cries reached my ears. Slanders, Dot hadn't cried like that in years. What had happened? Had Leo hurt her? No, I refused to believe that. But I'd left them alone together. What had caused Dot to cry in such pain?

A car door screeched open from the distant driveway.

"Dot?" a woman's voice called. My heart clenched as I recognized the voice. Mom? My heart lightened with the hope of her joining my dream. If Dot did, why not Mom too?

"Biddy!" Dad's footsteps pounded across the field to me as Rayban barked.

"Dot's hurt," I said, blindly gesturing the direction I'd come. Rayban, eager for praise at his job well done, sat beside me and sniffed my pockets for a treat.

Dad skidded in the dirt to run toward the continued cries. Dot's pain morphed into gasping breaths.

All fury at my sister shifted into fear. Was she alright?

The fear was partnered with frustration. Stepping off the porch and trying to find my way back to her would do nothing to help her. What could I do to help? I remained by the porch, gripping—squeezing the railing, listening for changes.

"Biddy!" Dad called. "Can you call the local doctor? He's closer and faster than the ER."

I shouted back that I would, then asked Rayban to help me inside to the house phone. I asked it to call the doctor who'd frequently helped me when I bumped into something more hazardous than the usual corners. I gave him brief details as Dot's sobs shuffled closer, accompanied by the voices of Mom and Dad.

"Do you think it's broken?" Mom asked.

Dad responded, "She'll need a doctor to know for sure, but it was definitely dislocated. Please, don't sue us."

"Heh," Mom laughed without humor. "The only winners in lawsuits are the lawyers."

With the doctor on his way, I ended the call and followed the whimpers of pain and worried voices to the guest room.

"The doctor said he'll be here in twenty minutes," I said. "What happened to Dot?"

"She only tripped—oh!" Mom said. "Uhh, who…"

"Yeah," Dad chuckled. "The resemblance is un-canny. This is my daughter, Biddy. I didn't catch your name."

"Candi," Mom said. An interesting nickname for my mom's full name, Candice. "Our daughters look like sisters."

Wait…then we weren't sisters in this dream world? Was Mom *not* my mom? That was a problem.

"What's your daughter saying?" Dad asked.

Mom translated Dot's signing, "She's asking what we're talking about. Lip reading is harder than the movies make it seem. I'll tell her the doctor's on his way."

"Wow," Dad said. "Sorry for staring, it's just…sign language is interesting to watch. My daughter's legally blind, so I know braille, but that's not considered its own language."

Mom scoffed with a light laugh. "ASL's a large factor of the Deaf culture. Would it help to elevate her foot? Or maybe wrap it with a wet rag? I've jammed my fingers more than once in my woodshop, and the doctor told me to use ice packs indirectly to help the swelling."

"Good idea. Biddy," Dad called to me. "Can you grab a hand towel? I'll grab the ice pack."

I nodded, glad to be of use. Dad returned first and took the towel from my extended hand with a, "Thanks." I remained at the doorway to stay out of the way, but too curious about Dot's situation to leave. I listened as Mom and Dad talked, working together to wrap and elevate Dot's foot. Satisfied that they'd done everything they could, he asked her, "You do woodshop?"

"Yeah. It started as a hobby, but became a necessary revenue after Dot's dad left."

Dad grunted with agreement. "I had to work twice as hard after Ruby's mom left me for the city-life."

Mom sighed. "Parenthood was never meant to be a one-person job."

"And single parents are left doing two jobs at once. You're good enough with woodworking to make a living with it? I'm impressed."

Were they…flirting? They were so timid about it, like they'd never met before. Weird.

Plots began to form. Could I match Mom and Dad? It seemed an odd thought as I also considered how to separate Dot from Leo and to match myself in his path instead.

I thought about it all day as the doctor came and reset Dot's foot. He still suggested they go to the Emergency Room to verify any possible broken bones. I listened as Mom and Dad teetered between flirting and worrying.

"We need to get her to the car," Mom said. "Would you help me with a two-handed seat carry?"

"Good idea. That'll keep any pressure off her foot. Here—oh, sorry. Which side did you want?"

"Doesn't matter. What's easiest for you?"

"I'm good wherever."

I internally gagged, almost glad I couldn't see their bitten back smiles and burning cheeks.

After a moment more of flustering, Dad said, "Grab my hand under her knees. Okay, and arms behind her back."

"Okay—oh!"

"Is something wrong?"

"No, just, um, your arms are…well, I can tell you work hard."

Words, parents were awkward.

They grunted and confirmed positioning as Dot moaned in pain between them, going back down the hallway, outside, and to their car.

Before closing the door to send them off, Dad said, "Call me if you need anything."

"I don't even know your name," Mom said.

"Eric. Here's my card with my number."

"Thank you, Eric. I'll give you an update when we know more—if anything because I'm sure Dot will want Leo to know."

As they drove off, Dad blew out a heavy breath and cursed. "I hope they don't sue us."

"Candi seemed nice enough," I said. It was weird to call my mom by her first name, especially a nickname.

We returned inside and my dad grabbed a snack and some water bottles for the workers. In the excitement, we hadn't prepared anything for their lunch. Odd to think that Dot visiting and breaking her foot would be the most "exciting" thing to happen around here. The oddest part was my realization that I had enjoyed the quiet farm life. No worries about the next inevitable attack from Huiess, about our reputations being soiled by sharing meals with hired helpers, or about keeping up appearances as a princess.

I missed my siblings, but considering my new anger at Dot, I mostly missed Mom.

"Dad?" I asked. "What if we let Dot and her mom stay with us until her foot heals?"

"Oh?"

"We aren't using the guest bedroom for anything else, and I miss having other women around." And I wanted my mom and dad to get together. But there was also the trick of keeping Leo away from Dot. I added, "But, since she's just lying there, immobile and defenseless, maybe we should be more strict on the rule about no workers coming into the house."

"She came all this way to see Leo."

"Especially Leo," I said. "Did you know they're engaged?"

Dad coughed on his food. "What—for marriage? How old are they?"

"Leo's eighteen and Dot's fifteen, the same age as I am."

"Don't you be getting any ideas. I'm surprised her mom allowed that. But you're right. Leo's not allowed in the house, and she's not allowed in his. Not on my property."

Excellent.

When Mom—Candi—called with news about Dot's condition, Dad asked her if she'd like to stay with us.

"Are you sure?" she asked over the phone. "Dot's stuck in a boot for at least the next six weeks. I wouldn't want to be in your way."

"Hey, the South isn't known for our hospitality by turning people away," Dad said. "I don't want your only experience in Texas to be a bad one. I promise no other harm will come to you if you stay here. You'll have your own room and good cooking for every meal."

I smiled, pleased with my dad's persuasion. When they returned, they spent most of the evening unloading Dot and the rest of their bags into the guest bedroom. We meant to have dinner with all four of us, but a thud then a howl erupted from Dot the moment she left the bed.

"Dot! What's wrong? Is your other foot broken too?"

Wails responded. Apparently there were also some hand signs, as Dad asked, "What's she saying?"

"She says she can't stand. Like there's a rock under her foot, and she can't put any pressure on it. Do we need to go back to the doctor's?"

"That looks like a 'No,'" Dad said.

"But you can't walk," Mom said, I assumed to Dot. "What are you going to do? Lie in bed all day?"

I didn't understand the rest of the conversation between the nonverbal body language, but that was exactly what Dot did.

Chapter 11

RUBY

Dad reiterated his rule about no workers in the main house. Leo grumbled and asked all the questions about Dot's well-being, which Dad happily answered. When he asked about visiting Dot, my dad chided, "Why do you think I just reminded everyone about the house rule?"

Leo was in a sour mood that evening, so I let the first day pass without trying to comfort him. Even still, most of his concerns were about Dot. How frustrating could she be?

In the meantime, I considered ways to make my mom and dad spend more time together. Dad invited her to join the rest of us for lunches on the patio, which was a good step. But then she grabbed Dot's plate and returned inside to spend it with Dot for the hour. After the second day of that, I volunteered to take Dot's plate inside. That let Mom spend the time with Dad while Rayban led me to Dot's room. There was no point staying with Dot since I had nothing to say to her, so I returned to the porch. Besides, lunches were my best time to chat with Leo, slowly distracting him from topics away from Dot.

A whole week passed like this. The local doctor visited to check on Dot, verifying that we were doing everything right to help her heal properly. With Mom, Dad, and the doctor crowding the room, I waited outside for the verdict. A bark from the driveway reminded me that the neighbor doctor usually kept his dog in the back of his truck.

"Rayban," I asked, "lead me to the truck."

My dog stepped forward, gently guiding me down the porch steps and straight across the wide driveway to the doctor's truck. Resting my hand against the sun-warmed metal, I slid my way to the back, where the barking increased.

"Hey, there," I said to the dog in the bed. "Calm down. Don't you know me? Be nice. I just want to pet you."

The dog's barking became an anxious whimper as I raised my hand for sniffing. Quick breathing warmed my hand as the dog sniffed me, then licked my fingers. I laughed and slid my hand around its face. Unlike Rayban, this dog had short fur around its squarish face and muscled body. It panted and thumped the truck with happy tail wagging as I rubbed around its ears.

The doctor's voice laughed from the porch. "I don't know how you do it, Biddy. Freckles doesn't get along with anyone outside my family except you."

"Maybe she's right about people. People can be the worst sometimes. On that topic, how's Dot?"

"She'll need at least six weeks to heal."

Six weeks. That seemed like a long time to be dreaming, but not enough time for Mom and Dad to be together. Would Mom stay here that long? I thanked the doctor and said bye to him and Freckles. Letting Rayban lead me back to the house, I considered how to use the next six weeks to my advantage.

I also felt the pressure to show my feelings for Leo. He had eventually stopped using every sentence to ask about Dot. He even laughed at my jokes sometimes. Maybe my plans were working.

In the middle of Dot's second week in Texas, she remained stuck in the guest bedroom, probably looking out the window, while I sat at the edge of the field, listening to the men work. I could pick out Leo's grunts and Shino's bursts of breath with every heavy action. Dot was somewhere inside. Maybe she watched the birds at the feeder. They seemed to be more active lately.

Yes, Dodo. Be happy with your silly little birds and leave Leo to me.

The lunch bell rang, and I waited for the men to pass me. I could pick out Leo by the smell of his sun lotion. Not that I would make a candle out of the scent, but it was better than sweat. Shino's scent was also decent with a hint of cinnamon, but it was Leo's that I followed. We ate side by side, and I laughed at his jokes, even when I didn't understand them. Mom did that with Dad, so I figured it was the right thing to do.

"Biddy," Mom said, "I'm a little trapped back here on this side of the bench. Would you mind grabbing one of everything for Dot's lunch plate?"

"Sure, Mom," I said. I didn't realize my mistake until the sudden stillness around me irritated my ears.

"Biddy," Dad said, his voice wavering with awkwardness. "She gave you a simple request. You didn't need to respond with sarcasm."

My tone hadn't been sarcastic at all, but what else could my dad say without making it more awkward? "Um, sorry," I said. "I hadn't meant to sound rude. It simply felt like the natural thing to say to you."

Why did I add "to you?" I was only making it worse. I wanted them to fall in love and marry to make this place feel more like home.

I cleaned my plate and filled a second for Dot, piling on the less-appetizing salad. But I wasn't completely vindictive. I added the nasty pickles on her hamburger, knowing how she liked them. I delivered her plate with Rayban's direction, then rejoined the workers to enjoy the conversations. Was it terrible to gloat a little that I could join them while Dot was stuck inside? Maybe.

As food was devoured and plates were scraped clean, I heard chairs scooting back to enjoy the remaining lunch hour before returning to the sun and fields.

Mom helped Dad to take the dishes inside for cleaning—something they never would have done as king and queen—and I took it as my chance.

Patting around the table until I found Leo's arm, I held his wrist. "Can you stay here with me a little longer?"

Leo shuffled in his seat, twisting and loosening his arm slightly from my hold. "I have to get back to work."

"The lunch hour isn't over. And I only wanted a few minutes," I said.

"Uh, did you have something to say?"

"Not really. I hoped to feel you," I said. In a rush, I clarified, "I mean, I have my own image of you, but I'd like to know what you look like. May I touch you?"

"Uhh," he drawled, his tone uncomfortable and unsure.

"It's not awkward unless you make it awkward. I like to know what my friends look like," I said, hoping to reassure him. Even if I called him my friend, my heart knew better.

My hand reached for him, slowly extending until it bumped into something solid. Rock solid. He was as muscled as I remembered from our first meeting. I spread my fingers against the fabric of his shirt, feeling the cold dampness of his labor. My hand kept searching for his face, going up and up… Words, he was tall!

He must have noticed my stretching as he lowered himself. The table groaned under his weight, but we were about eye-level. My hands slid outward, following the curves of his broad shoulders, before curling back in and up his thick neck. The more I discovered about him, the more I realized how massive he truly was.

My hands jumped a little with surprise when they ran into his unshaven neck. He had a full beard which hung a half inch off of his chin. His hair was coarse individually, but cushioned as a whole. I could still feel the leanness of his jawbone. Going up to his ears, I was surprised again by his hair. It was long enough to tie up into a man-bun.

"What color is your hair?" I asked.

"Brown," he said. "Do you know what brown looks like?"

I smirked. "I know."

"You weren't born blind?"

"No," I said. Dad said I lost my sight a few years ago from an accident. While my memories of Ormio blurred, I also had memories of the accident when I went too close to a green tractor in harvest.

I shifted back to Leo's face, rolling over his narrow cheekbones, sharp nose with a little bump below his bridge, and over his thick eyebrows.

"What color are your eyes?"

"Light brown."

I smiled at the completed image of him in my head. He was a bit of an animal, but a handsome one.

Before I knew it, I was feeling his lips. They were scratchy and chapped from the day in the sun and tasted salty.

Leo's large hands enveloped my shoulders and pushed me back. "Ruby!"

Oh. That wasn't with my hands.

"I'm engaged! Just because you look like my fiancée doesn't mean you can kiss me."

"My feelings for you have nothing to do with Dot," I said.

"My feelings have everything to do with Dot."

His words were like a slap to my heart. Did that mean he had no feelings at all for me? No, it couldn't be. He must have misunderstood.

"Leo, I love you," I whispered.

I held my breath as I waited for him to respond. He heard me, right? He was suddenly as silent as Shino, but who knew with his hearing loss? Did I need to say it again?

No, he took a sharp breath in, as if preparing his lungs for some great exclamation.

"I think you're confused."

I filtered through his words, hurt that he hadn't said "I love you" back. The more I pondered on his reply, the worse it became. He didn't say "I don't love you." No, he called me "confused" like a crazy loon. Not only did he say that he didn't love me, but he discounted my confession. He called my feelings fake.

My cheeks grew hot. I turned and stumbled back into the house as tears welled in my useless eyes.

I skipped the next day of lunch, choosing to drown my sorrows in chips and salsa with intense flavorings that reminded me of Huiess. Slanders, this food was good, and the spices were distracting enough to help me forget about Leo for a glorious second after every bite.

Let Dodo have him for all I cared. I didn't need him. Forget about him. Stop thinking about him. Why was I still thinking about him? Slanderous brain, why wouldn't it listen to me?

Rayban whined and placed his chin on my leg. Maybe he was begging for food, or maybe he sensed my distress and wanted to comfort me. I pat his head while biting down on another salsa-loaded chip.

My eyes burned, and my nose leaked. Words, why was it hard to breathe? Was it the spices? They were the kind of hot that blowing on them didn't change anything, but I found myself chewing with my mouth open to take heavier breaths between bites.

Hey, look at that. I stopped thinking about Leo for five whole seconds. A great excuse to load my next chip with a heavy helping of salsa.

Muffled sobs escaped from the guest bedroom. Dot. When I initially touched Leo's face, I'd hoped she was watching. After Leo's rejection, however, I imagined her celebrating. Why was she crying? She had Leo. It didn't seem fair for her to cry when I was the one heartbroken.

Shutting myself in my room, I hoped to hide away from her tears. Could I still wake up and realize this was all a dream? It didn't feel like a dream. I never hurt like this before, dreaming or not. I was fairly certain that there was no waking up, no undo, no reset.

I sobbed into my own pillow, remembering the good days when Dot and I practiced duets with our instruments, playing in front of the entire masquerade crowds to impress a single man, when we bickered over little things that were easily forgiven and forgotten by the morning. I missed the times when Mom and Dia would listen to us and help us rationalize away our feelings, when Cephas challenged me to a game of Knights and Pawns, or when Opal could make me a "lucky" bracelet to make it all better.

But Dot's mom didn't know me, and my other siblings weren't here. I felt…blind without them.

I listened to a book to mentally escape this dream world, but the characters reminded me too much of Leo. Sleep was a relief, but only for so long. I dreamed of memories with Dot taking everything I wanted—always arriving first, being praised first, choosing the first rewards, leaving me with seconds, seconds, seconds.

I dreamed of Leo and Dot dancing at the masquerades, of them laughing in a carriage ride through Veriae, holding hands during a stroll through the gardens. They told me in every way but words, "Dot won. Dot beat you. Dot doesn't need you. No one needs you. You don't belong here."

I woke with an aching heart, pounding and miserable. Moisture covered my face, but I couldn't tell if it was sweat or tears. Maybe both.

Asking Siri for the time, I realized I'd slept through dinner and the night. Slanders, no wonder I was hungry like a wolf.

I went to the kitchen to stuff my face with every bready sweet in the house. As if filling my stomach could fill the hole in my heart. When we ran out, I pulled ingredients to make sweet biscuits.

I ate until my stomach hurt and Mom came from the guest bedroom.

"Biddy, we missed you at dinner. You must be starving. What are you making?"

"Biscuits."

"Okay," she said. "Did you see the leftovers in the fridge? I put them in the usual spot, as your dad requested."

"No," I lied. Honestly, I shook the container and smelled the vegetable soup, then craved anything else.

"Come on, you should eat something healthy."

The smell of creamed butter and sugar taunted me all the more, but I knew Mom wouldn't let me continue.

I grumbled. "Maybe I'm not as hungry as I thought."

"Nah-ah," Mom scolded. "I see those granola wrappers in the trash. Hungry or not, you should eat something with vegetables."

Grumbling more did nothing to dissuade her. Technically, she wasn't my mom, but I didn't have the gumption to disobey her on that principle. Admittedly, the soup wasn't terrible, but I was stuffed full after half a bowl.

"I can't eat another bite," I said, nudging the soup bowl away from me.

"Alright. How about we cover the biscuit mix to finish making them for the men's lunch?"

"Sure." And that was what we did. The workers seemed extra excited as we served the biscuits with homemade jam and the fixings to put together their own ham sandwiches.

I went to my usual spot by my dad, but found it taken by Dot's mom. Oh, right. I'd arranged that. But where did that leave me?

"Miss Fashingbauer," Shino said, using my Texas surname, "you can sit over here."

"Thanks," I said. "Rayban, can you guide me over to Shino?"

My ever-present dog pressed his nose to my fingers, letting my hand slide up his face, over his neck and back, then pulled me in the direction of the open seat. I sat, and Rayban took his usual spot beside me.

"Miss Fashingbauer, you have a good dog," Shino said in his broken English. Though it sounded less and less broken with each passing day.

"Yes," I said, "he's well trained. And, please, call me Biddy." Maybe if I accepted the dream name, I could become someone new—someone who didn't hurt like I did.

"Biddy?" Shino asked with a small voice. "Do you feel better today?"

Feel better? Had Dad told everyone I was sick? Or had Shino seen my tears?

"I feel well enough," I lied.

"Good," he said, and I heard the smile in his voice. What did his smile look like?

That thought reminded me of feeling Leo's face, killing any desire to join the lunch-time conversations.

When lunch finished, Shino said farewell with a practiced, "See you later, Biddy." Mom and I took the dishes inside.

"Biddy," Mom said, "Dot has asked to talk privately with you. Your dad says you have a phone app that does text-to-speech so you could talk, then she can read and text back. She seemed really eager to talk with you."

No doubt about that. I also had a few words to share.

She escorted me to the guest bedroom, and we were greeted with a tuneless shout.

"Dot?" Mom asked. "What's wrong? OK, OK, I'll leave you two alone."

As soon as her footsteps left the room, rustling from the bed told me that Dot was moving furiously, despite her bad leg.

Pulling up my text-to-speech note-taking app, I smirked and asked, "You wanted to talk to me?"

I handed her the phone to let her read the text, then respond.

With the voice of Siri, Dot said, "I saw you."

"Good."

My sister's bed creaked with a quick gesture.

I added, "I want Leo."

Dot shouted with an off-pitch moan until Siri spoke, "Stop wanting everything that's mine. It doesn't matter what you have, you always want whatever I have."

"I do not!" I argued. "You always take whatever I want!"

"Lies. When you won the flower arrangements competition, you won the most beautiful hat while I got a hair ribbon for third place. You never wore your hat, but stole my ribbon on multiple occasions."

"It went better with my hair! And you know how I hate hats!"

Dot moaned for my phone to translate again. Of course, she couldn't let me have the last word.

"Stop trying to be me," she said through Siri. "If you weren't so busy stealing my boyfriend, we'd be back home and this miserable nightmare would be over."

"I'm not trying to be you," I snapped with disgust. "I hate hats because I want everyone to see my hair and how I'm different from you! I want to be better than you!"

Determined to have the last word, I turned on my heel and marched out the door—almost hitting it. Thankfully, Rayban was there to guide me through. I went to my own room and slammed the door behind me.

That night, I dreamed of sneaking to Noz Isle's midnight masquerade on our usual little sailboat. Opal wore all her lucky bracelets and necklace charms, jingling with her every movement. Dia stared ahead at the island, eager to see her friends from the other kingdoms. My sisters and I laughed and teased each other about the men we'd dance with, excited about the friends we'd see. Reaching the island, we raced up the stairs to the castle and the great ballroom.

I stood in the entrance, basking in the sight of the great chandeliers, tables of food, and a talented orchestra. The amount of people made my heart tense with anxiety, but then I found the familiar masks of the Somnus and Huiess Princesses. My heart ached to see my friends. I'd missed them more than I thought.

In the time I'd been distracted, Dot had already picked a partner. It was Leo as I imagined him to be;

156

so tall and rock solid. Even though I had a good sense of his face now, it was hidden behind a lion's mask.

The song seemed to play with never ending repetition as I watched. They danced around and around, laughing together, passing me over and over. Sometimes they blatantly stared at me as they skipped by. Other times, they ignored me like I didn't exist. I didn't know which was worse.

Furious, I marched up to them as they came near for the hundredth time. They stopped, asking what I wanted. As if they couldn't tell.

I shoved Dodo away from Leo and pulled him into a dance with me. It was time for my sister to watch with her perfect vision. Leo danced with me, but his laughter was gone. I waited for my fury to fade, for my anger to turn sweet with revenge. Instead, my fake joy felt soured with guilt.

Turning back to Dot, I found her dancing with Shino, or at least a man I imagined as the quiet worker. When had he arrived? His long-nosed mask covered everything except his eyes, that watched me and Leo with sad longing. Beside him, Dot stared with the same pain.

Their pain reflected back and bit into me. I screamed as someone laughed with wicked glee. Did I recognize that voice? It reminded me of one of the Somnus princesses—no, the grandma—no, the wolf!

There wasn't time to think as the pain bit down again, piercing my neck. My vision became swallowed by darkness. Dot screamed for me in the background. I remembered feeling hope when Dot shouted for me even as the wolf attacked me at the cabin. Dot would help me, save me, be there for me like she always had been.

This time, when she screamed, there was no hope.

PART 2

"Then she went to the bed and drew back the curtains…
No sooner had the wolf spoken those words than he
leaped out of bed and gobbled up poor
Little Red Cap…
'Oh, how terrified I was!
It was so dark in the wolf's belly!'"

– *Little Red Cap*, by Brothers Grimm

Chapter 12

EMER

With her window cracked open to Denebrae's streets, Emer woke to the sound of early risers and their morning routines. Breathing deeply, she stretched on the comfortable mattress of the mermaid inn, reluctant to rise until thoughts of Caden fed her with energy. Shuffling on the overdress that Jesse had altered for her, she braided her blonde hair into a tail for their later travels. Quietly to let Pearl continue sleeping, Emer poked her head from her room and spied into the inn's main area. The room was empty save for a man shuffling through Caden's book bag hanging on the wall.

"What are you doing?" she asked, stepping out to confront the sneak.

Leo flinched and snapped his hands back from Caden's pack. A book of notes fell to the ground.

Leo said nothing as Emer slowly approached. He worked his jaw as his eyes darted to the ground, but otherwise stood tall and motionless.

Emer picked up the fallen book. It was Caden's research on the individual princesses. Emer weighed the book in her hand and studied the former Prince of Braeder. "You know," she said, "if you wanted to know something about me, my sisters, or friends, you could have asked."

He swallowed heavily, but said nothing.

"Hmm?" Emer prodded. "Shall we take a look?" She opened the book, but merely glanced at it between her analysis of Leo's reactions. "It seems that Caden organized us by age. The eldest is Garnet, my sister, and rightful ruler of Somnus." No reaction. "Then Amethyst, the rightful ruler of Huiess. We all called her Ame." No change from Leo. "Aquamarine, whom you know as Marin, then Diamond—or Dia, the rightful heir of Ormio." Nothing. "Then we have me and Pearl…"

She paused to study him extra hard. She expected him to be most reluctant to admit researching her, though he almost seemed relieved at her suspicion. Emer turned a couple more pages to pass Caden's meticulous notes on her. "Then we have the Ormio twins, Ruby and Peri—ah-hah!"

Emer pointed and grinned when Leo twitched at the twins' names. "Tell me, Prince Leo of Braeder, what interest do you have in the Ormio twins?"

He coughed, swallowed again, and looked at the book like it was an apple he wanted to steal from the market.

"Come on," Emer urged. "My mother taught me that someone who asks a question is a fool for one minute, but someone who never asks is a fool forever."

His eyes finally met hers and darkened. "I am no fool."

"Then ask away."

Only after taking and releasing a deep breath, he asked, "How would you describe the twins?"

"In what way?" she asked, prodding for his level of curiosity. "Their appearances, personalities, or habits?"

He said nothing at first, but Emer wasn't afraid of silence. She would wait until he gave an answer.

Grumbling a little, he relented. "Whatever."

Emer raised her eyebrows. That hadn't been a "nevermind" kind of "whatever." It had been a "tell me anything" kind.

All the more curious, she said, "They were opposites of the same coin. While they look very similar, Ruby was named for her redder hair, and Peridot was named for her greener eyes. They both have bold personalities, confident, and without a care of what others think of them." Emer recalled more than one example at the Noz Isle midnight masquerades. The twins occasionally asked to borrow a horn and flute from the musicians to perform duets in front of the entire audience. Emer squirmed with anxiety and jealousy of their confidence. Following their performance, they often ran to a man to ask what he thought. Continuing to Leo, Emer said, "They were opposites in everything except for the things they wanted. They often wanted the same thing at the same time, but they never wanted to share. Especially concerning men."

Leo grunted, as if agreeing.

"Did you have something to add?"

"Was Dot deaf?"

"Deaf?" Emer raised her eyebrows again. "No, but...how did you know Peridot's nickname?"

He shied his face away.

"Leo?" she prodded. "What are you not telling me?"

With another heavy swallow, he said, "I don't normally remember my dreams after waking... But the one from last night won't go away."

Emer tilted her head and waited patiently for him to continue. She could have waited all day, but rustling behind Caden and Mica's door distracted Leo's attention. Emer refused to let the conversation drop. She had her suspicions for why the subject made him uneasy, but she had to confirm. "Tell me, Leo. What did you dream about?"

His eyes darted like a spooked rabbit. His shoulders hunched forward, and he whispered in his extra loud voice, "The twins. They were in my dream last night."

"Both of them?" Emer asked. That was new. Even though she and Pearl had dreamed of the same people, it hadn't been at the same time. Marin and Ranae had shared a dream, though they'd been poisoned nearly the same time. "Were they in England?"

Leo shook his head. "It was some place called Tessas. Or something. There were yellow flat farming fields for miles around, like upper Uldra, but I kept thinking how it was nothing like the area of Washton where I grew up. None of it makes any sense. I'd brush it off as a crazy dream…but it felt so real, and how could I dream of the twins when I've never met them?"

Emer reviewed her many travels during her dreams, but never passed any flat farming fields. All the fields she saw in England had been green hills.

"Either you were set somewhere beyond the places I visited," she said, "or somewhere beyond England entirely. I recall Caden mentioning other kingdoms across the seas. On another topic, there is the issue of timing. Caden and Mica only started dreaming after waking Pearl and me. Could this mean that Ruby and Dot are awake?"

Leo nodded. "I get the sense that something changed for one of them, but I don't know which one, and…" His voice drifted and his stoicism returned. "We need to find them. You wake the women, I'll wake the men."

That, at least, was their next step. Returning to her room, Emer urged Pearl awake, hearing the men stir and pack. The innkeeper and his wife wouldn't let them leave without a full breakfast, letting the sun rise completely before Emer and her friends saddled their horses and packed the carriage.

Walking down the streets and waving to peeking passersby, Emer asked Leo, "Have you told Caden about your dream of Ruby and Dot?"

Caden's attention snapped to Leo as the former Prince of Braeder clenched his teeth and turned hard eyes on Emer. She grinned back.

"What's this?" Caden asked, rummaging for his notes. "You dreamed of the Ormio twins?"

Leo grumbled, but began his story. "I dreamed of being in a land called Tessas, or something like that. I was a hired hand, working the fields owned by Ruby's parents. Dot was there, but I only saw her through the house's back window."

Emer frowned. "How did you know it was Dot, not Ruby?" They looked identical from a distance.

"She saw me," Leo said. "Ruby was blind, and Dot was deaf. I made hand signals to Dot from the window, and she responded."

"Interesting," Caden said, taking notes. "It seems each princess loses a sense in their dreams. Emer lost her sense of touch, Pearl lost her sense of taste, Ruby lost her sight, and Peridot lost her hearing? Marin's loss of her teeth doesn't fit the pattern as nicely, but her husband also shared her dream and was turned into a frog. Then again, people dream of losing their teeth all the time. We all experience losing our baby teeth, and sometimes the memories haunt our dreams."

His voice drifted as he rambled and wrote down his thoughts. They rode in silence for a bit until Caden paused in his note-taking and frowned.

"What confuses me," he said, "is that I dreamt of Emer, and Mica dreamt of Pearl. None of us dreamt of Marin, but her husband was with her. It seems that we share the dreams of our lovers, but if that's the case, why did you, of all people, dream of both Ormio twins?"

Emer watched for Leo's answer with her own suspicions.

Leo grunted—or was it an uncomfortable cough? His jaw clenched, but…was that red around his neck?

Caden raised an eyebrow. "Huh, that's a new look for you."

"Beshrew you," Leo cursed, and urged his horse ahead.

Caden laughed. "So, you have options. Which princess won the stony heart of Leo Bahr?" He raised his voice to follow Leo's departing figure, shouting across the group with his last words.

Emer watched him huff ahead, bewildered.

They had almost reached the edge of the town when a voice called from the right, "Stop!"

Emer urged Caden to direct their horse over, but paused when Leo raised a hand to halt them. He dismounted and crept forward with his bow in hand. Shinópu jumped from the carriage with his two curved swords, and followed him.

"Wait!" the voice cried again as two people and a horse appeared from between the houses. They were about middle-aged, a man jogging beside a woman on the horse. The man was stocky, like Shinópu and Thachuma, but had dark brown hair instead of black. His bulbous nose could have been broken, but his well-groomed beard and clothes suggested a less rambunctious lifestyle. He packed away a strange device that reminded Emer of cellphones. She could have sworn it glowed before he released it.

The woman on the horse looked even more peculiar. Her thick brunette hair fell around her face with wild waves, and she wore a paradoxical style of clothes that were fine fabrics frayed with layers in unexpected places.

Shinópu sheathed his swords, but Leo remained focused on the newcomers.

"Name yourselves," Leo called.

The woman pulled the horse to a stop, and the man snapped his hands up in surrender.

"Uh, thanks for waiting," he said with a deep bass. "We are travelers from Faenor, recently from Uldra. People call me Charger, and this is my wife, Brooke."

Strange names for strange people. If they were from Faenor, they were from the kingdom on the western side of the Ezuthithe Caves and mountains. They hardly looked equipped to travel such a long distance, even if they stopped in Uldra.

Charger examined Shinópu, Emer, and Caden. "Fantastic! It looks like we found you in time."

"You were looking for us?" Emer asked, while Leo growled, "In time for what?"

"For the revolution," he said. "We traveled from Uldra after hearing that the princes of the grassland kingdoms were here, waking a princess from a deep sleep and freeing the slaves of an ogress. Well done, you."

Caden frowned. "Who told you this?"

Charger looked back to his wife for confirmation. "That bullbegging man, Goth, I think was his name. Then, this morning, we heard you made a stir in town. Something about a revolution in Rezhina."

"Gother?" Shinópu asked.

Brooke snapped her fingers and pointed at Shinópu as if he won something. "That's the one! Gother! What a total forfended nincompoop. Heard him tell the whole Uldran court about how you offed the ogress princess. He got the ogres in a total uproar. They ripped the treaty draft and reclaimed war. Lucky for the Uldrans, the ogres split their army to send a whole battalion after you guys."

"Lucky for the Uldrans?" Caden echoed, while Pearl went a tint whiter.

"After us?" she squeaked.

"Yep," Brooke said. "That's why we were worried about reaching you guys in time. We could travel faster than the whole battalion, but then that Gother guy took an elite group to go ahead. Looks like you survived the first wave."

Shinópu stared like a sentinel at the east and nodded solemnly. "Gother warned me."

Leo took notice and followed the dwarf prince's gaze. "Beshrews," he cursed.

"More ogres are coming after us?" Emer asked, trying to catch the meaning behind the two fighters' worry and—dare she say—fear.

"Before he died," Shinópu said, "Gother said, 'More will come.'"

"More?" Marin asked. "We nearly died multiple times from that attack."

Caden joined their vigil eastward. "Are those fires? That can't be good."

"Ogres," Leo spat like it was another curse.

"Safe to say," Emer said, "they are unhappy with us about Charlotte. I thought she said something about the ogres having a treaty with Tanzi to leave this land alone. It looks like they ripped that apart too for vengeance on us."

"On you," Marin clarified. "Ranae, Pearl, and I had nothing to do with your ogres mess."

Pearl pouted her puffy lips. "Mica's problems are my problems. I want to help him to regain the Zubra kingdom."

"Ah," Brooke spoke up, "speaking of regaining the grassland kingdoms, the dwarves took the castle skirmish as a sign to finally come out of hiding. Did you know," she asked, pointing at Shinópu, "that the dwarves went underground—like literally—to escape the war? We had no idea, but you know, it makes sense."

Charger winked at his wife. "There was no way the dwarves were overcome that easily. I figured they went into hiding, but no one knew where."

"Underground," Shinópu whispered. "They escaped after all."

Emer watched as the former prince's tension melted off of him, relaxing his shoulders with undeniable relief. Pearl stepped up beside him and rested a hand on his dropped shoulder.

She smiled at him sadly. "Did you want to join them?"

Caden scoffed with a mixed chuckle. "Join them? He'd be better off leading them."

"What a brilliant idea!" Charger said. "We shall escort you north!"

Shinópu took two eager steps forward, ready to go.

Emer's insides panicked. Shinópu had been one to defend their search for her friends. His support for Caden had influenced Jesse and Thachuma's, convincing Leo to continue with them despite his arguments that their search was a waste of time. Mica had mostly defended their search because he was fixated on Pearl.

With Pearl awake, Jesse and Thachuma heading north with Hanzo, and Shinópu ready to join his people, was it time to return to Uldra to fight the ogres? Caden had come to Rezhina looking for an army by appealing to the leaders—either Queen Tanzi or Garnet as the rightful heir. If the dwarves rejoined the fight, they wouldn't need Rezhina's army.

Would they abandon the search for the other princesses? Emer assumed that Marin and Ranae would continue the search, but Pearl would probably follow Mica, who would probably follow Caden. If the treaty was torn, then he could return home without fear of another arranged marriage. If ever they were to return to support Uldra against the ogres, this was the time.

Emer studied Caden's face as he frowned in thought, eyes bouncing between each member of their group. He had probably made similar conclusions, and now waited for the next player to move.

Leo groaned and clawed at his hair. "This had to happen now?"

Emer blinked in surprise. She had expected Leo to jump as eagerly as Shinópu to fight the ogres. Instead, he grimaced like a man torn between choices. Again, she wondered exactly what had happened in his dream of the Ormio twins.

"Shinópu," Caden said, "you're not a prisoner among us. You may leave if you wish, but it's been years since your family was known among the dwarves. Will they let you lead them?"

The quiet prince pondered for a second, then gave a half shrug. "Maybe they accept my leadership. Maybe not. Either way, I want to help them. But you freed me from the ogress. I also want to help you."

Caden responded with a small smile. "If you fight for Uldra, you are helping me. You honor us regardless."

Shinópu accepted that with a nod.

Caden released a heavy breath, eying his volumes of notes. "If there's a battalion of ogres after Emer and me, I'm afraid the best thing I can do for Uldra is to lead that battalion as far away from Uldra as possible. Yes, we'll lead the ogres through Rezhina Valley, but we've traveled only through unpopulated areas until Denebrae."

"Oh, don't worry about Denebrae," Brooke said. "We warned the mayor and town council this morning. They're totally confident that they can divert the ogres around them."

"Good," Caden said with a nod. "Leo, will you join Shinópu?"

Emer watched as the former Prince of Braeder struggled to keep his expression stoic between his frustrations.

Looking between Caden and Mica, he said, "I now understand why you were so eager to find the princesses of Rezhina. Dot and Ruby need us, and each princess we wake gives us a new magical power

174

and influence over the valley. I can't abandon them, even if it means neglecting my people."

Caden steered his horse to step beside Leo, allowing Caden to reach down and clap his hand on the large man's shoulder. "We could surely use your help if we come against that army of ogres."

Leo returned him the stink-eye. "You'd be a fool to let that happen."

"Indeed." Caden smirked. "I hate to rush goodbyes, but it seems we have an army to outrun and a couple of princesses to wake. Thank you, Charger and Brooke, for your timely information. Shinópu," Caden paused to smile gratefully. "You weren't born to be a slave or to follow others. You're the Prince of Chafan. Go prove it. For Chafan and Uldra."

"For Zubra!" Mica added with a fist in the air.

"For Braeder," Leo growled. "Take my horse. He's fast and accustomed to battle. I'd ask you to save some ogres for me to kill, but with my own battalion on our heels, I think that'll be enough for me."

Shinópu said nothing as he gave their group a small smile and bow. Then, he mounted Leo's massive horse and joined Charger and Brooke.

Charger turned northward, but angled back for a wave. "Please, take care. Faenor roots for you."

"Totally," the strange woman said. "We'll need to hurry to reach Uldra, and they'll need to hurry to escape the ogres. I expect the battalion's only a day away."

Charger mounted behind his wife, then the three of them dashed away. Marin settled inside the carriage while Leo took the seat beside Ranae on top.

Emer urged Caden to steer his horse to catch up to the former Prince of Braeder. "Leo—"

"Don't talk to me," he grumbled.

She wanted to argue, but Caden paused her with a hand on her arm. "Don't push him. The Braeder people aren't the type to talk about their issues, no matter how conflicted they may be." He ended with a raised eyebrow at Leo, as if to challenge him, but the gruff prince said nothing.

Chapter 13

EMER

No one spoke as they continued south without Shinópu. Despite the dwarf prince's quiet presence, his vacancy left a deeper silence. Emer analyzed the downcast expressions of Leo, Caden, and Mica. They all wished to return to Uldra and fight for their kingdoms, yet it was safer for them and their people to lead the battalion of ogres on a merry chase away from Uldra. They rode with a maintained canter, hoping to gain ground and keep their distance between them and the oncoming ogres. They occasionally slowed the horses to a trot. Injuring a horse in their haste would severely delay them, and no one was willing to take that risk, especially Marin.

They stopped for meals and to rest the horses, eventually easing back into their usual conversations and banter. As long as they didn't look back at the nearing fires, they could forget the ogres chasing them.

On their third day away from Denebrae, Emer expected to reach the Western Bridge between Somnus and Ormio.

"Maybe," Emer said to Caden over his shoulder, "we can lose the ogres over the bridge. Its depth and width make it impossible to cross without the bridge or a boat. They will be bottlenecked there."

"It's a good idea. We need to cross it anyway to reach the other princesses in Ormio."

Thankfully, their horses had been trained for long travels, allowing them to switch between intermittent runs, trots, and canters. Still, they stopped to rest and eat lunch when reaching the origins of Lake Imazhin from the mountain rivers.

Marin directed the water to flow pure where the horses bent for a drink, and Emer grew grass for their feed.

Caden and Mica huddled together, looking over a map. "We still have a couple kilometers west along the river until we come to the bridge. With our pace, I think we can spare another half hour for the horses."

"Hardly enough time," Marin muttered.

"I know," Ranae said. "But if the horses are too slow, they become ogre food like the rest of us."

Meanwhile, Leo sharpened and shined his weapons in preparation for battle. Emer dearly hoped it wouldn't come to that.

One of the horses jerked its face from the water and stomped its front hooves before backing from the shore. Another one pulled away, its ears flicking back and forth.

Caden frowned and grabbed the reins of his temperamental horse. "Hey, Tucker, what's gotten into you? Is something in the water? Princess Aquamarine?"

Marin stared at the section of water that she cleared for the horses and shook her head.

"Ho, there," Ranae called, pointing farther into the lake. "Those waves are unnatural."

The mist obscured anything farther than a kilometer away, but Emer could pick out intermittent waves on the water surface.

"Marin," she asked. "Can you tell what is in the water?"

"I do not know, can I?"

Caden frowned. "Is this a 'can I' versus 'may I' issue? Either way, I think it's time to go. The horses seem anxious to move on."

Indeed, every horse nervously backed away from the water's edge. A couple of the coach horses tossed their heads, ripping the reins from Ranae's hands.

"Is it just me," Ranae asked, regaining the reins and pulling himself to the coach driver's seat, "or are those waves moving back and forth?"

No one answered as they were all too busy climbing onto their horses. The ground trembled beneath Emer's feet before Caden reached down to help her into the saddle behind him. There was no time to adjust her skirts to make sure they covered her ankles. The thunder of a thousand footsteps grew in the air.

"Ride!" Caden said, snapping his horse into movement.

Emer lost the sound of footsteps beneath the galloping horses. She hoped their speed would keep them ahead of the ogres. This wasn't a battle they could fight. They could only run.

Emer wrapped her arms around Caden's waist as his horse leapt into a quick canter. The others followed closely behind in slow gallops. They ran along the right side of the wide pathway, closer to the forest.

"Come on," Caden muttered to his horse. "I know you're spooked about the water, but you can't keep pulling to the right. The ogres are on the right, and the bridge will be on the left."

Emer looked back to see the others having similar struggles with their horses. The carriage rolled at hazardous speeds off of the trail as the four horses drove it far to the right.

With her eyes backward and to the right, she caught movement among the trees. Shadows flicked in and out between the trees over an entire acre. She squinted, trying to follow a single object long enough to catch what it was. When she did, she gasped and hugged herself tighter to Caden.

"Whatever you do," she said, "keep going."

"Why?"

Before she could answer, an ogre roared from the forest to their right. Several more joined it until there were too many to count.

"Devils," Caden swore, and snapped his reins to urge his horse into a running gallop.

They kept this pace for a couple of minutes, but the horses grew tired. Caden allowed them to slow, but the ogres gained on them. The army came closer to the river where the trees thinned and they ran with fewer obstructions. There were so many—at least a hundred, maybe a couple hundred—that they blended into one another. Emer could hardly keep her eyes off of them as they charged, their green skin blending between the trees. She best distinguished them from their wooden armor that was held together with metal rims and bolts. Most of it was dyed red, or at least, Emer hoped it was paint and dyes.

"There's the bridge!" Caden called back.

Emer forced her eyes away from the ogres to spot the Western Bridge ahead that crossed the Imazhin River. The great stone bridge had thankfully been updated and kept strong over the past hundred harvests as an important crossway between Somnus and Ormio. With the kingdoms now dissolved, it was still a necessary path between the north and south sides of Lake Imazhin.

Caden tugged, then pulled on his horse to angle left. It continued to go straight, leaning toward the ogres on the right.

"What's wrong?" Caden growled. "Whatever spooked you in the water can't be worse than the ogres!"

"Ranae?" Marin called from inside the carriage to her husband. "What are those?"

Emer followed her older sister's gaze to the water's edge that boiled without steam. Large black bubbles rose from the river surface until Emer realized they weren't bubbles at all. They were heads. Black heads, shaped like horses, but growling with long, dagger-like teeth. Instead of manes, they had jagged black fins going down their necks and spines. Their bodies were all black and scaled like dragons. They rose out of the water on powerful hind legs, but their thick tails fanned vertically like sharks.

There were perhaps a hundred of them emerging from the water and glaring at Emer and her company.

"Devils of the southern hills," Caden cursed, his whispered voice shaking. Then, he roared, "Run!"

Before Emer could ask why, he snapped his reins, over and over, feverishly urging his horse to go faster.

"What?" Emer asked, holding onto him as best as she could. "What are they?"

Caden's answer was simply to lean forward, as if they could escape the monsters on their left and right simply by ducking. She barely caught a glance backward to make sure the others followed. No one else seemed as terrified as Caden, but no one else seemed to know what they were running from. Still, they raced ahead.

"Maybe we can lose them in the tunnels," Caden shouted over the galloping.

"The Ezuthithe Caves?" Ranae shouted back. "Is that really our best option?"

"It's our only option!" Caden said.

Pearl whimpered. "There are stories of a dragon living inside."

"The stories of the monsters chasing us are far worse!" Caden said, urging his horse even more, passing the bridge that was surrounded with black scaled bodies. The black monsters crawled from the shore, following Emer's passing with lightless eyes.

Emer looked back, green and red on their right and black on their left.

"I see the cave entrance!" Mica shouted.

"Hurry!" Caden said. "They might follow us inside, but at least they'll be forced to fight us one-on-one."

"And what," Leo asked, "will we be fighting?"

Emer turned back again. The ogres were within a stone's throw, but everyone was too busy running to aim. They passed the black water monsters as more continued to stand from the water. The first row of sea monsters joined the chase. Emer's muscles clenched with terror as they moved faster than any creature she'd seen, leaving a smoky image in their wake. The mass of black merged into the green.

If she tuned her ears beyond the pounding of the hooves and her own heart, she heard shouts from the ogres. Not the roars of a charge, but…screams.

"What are they?" Marin asked.

They reached the cave mouth, and Caden finally pulled his horse to slow down. The poor animals heaved for breath as Caden dismounted and nearly yanked Emer off after him. The two forces of monsters had paused on the river road for a skirmish—no, a battle. Emer spotted the dark figures shifting like ghosts between the red and green tones of the ogres.

An ogre broke away from the main body, coming closer. Emer's heart leapt with fear before she noticed the outright terror on its face. If the ogre made it to her, she doubted it would have attacked her. It would have spared her no second thought during its insane urge to run away.

It had no chance of reaching Emer and her friends.

One of the black creatures caught it from behind, slashing with no weapons that Emer could see. It struck the ogre down with a single swipe of its massive claws between webbed fingers.

Its soulless eyes found her staring, and it roared with determined hate.

In that moment, Emer thought she had met Death. Then, she corrected herself.

No, this thing is not Death. This creature is the reason Death hides under cloaks and carries a reaping weapon for defense.

The creature started to blur toward them, bellowing its anger, showing off its long pointed teeth…like needles.

Caden grabbed Emer's arm, jolting her from the terrifying stupor. He stopped under the cave mouth, but swung Emer into the darkness.

"Come on!" he yelled at the others. Other black nightmares answered the call of the first and began to ignore the ogres to run after Emer and her friends.

They ran with blurring speeds, leaving ghostly shadows behind.

The carriage arrived, and Caden waved at Marin and Ranae. "Leave the carriage! Into the cave! Now!"

Emer grabbed their vine phone from the carriage to leave one end at the cave entrance. She uncoiled it and peered around the cave edge as Mica and Pearl, then Marin and Ranae ran inside.

The ogres had stopped screaming. Instead, gurgled cries like drowning horses echoed closer.

Leo stopped at the cave's edge to turn around and aim an arrow at the oncoming creatures.

"Inside!" Caden demanded, grabbing Leo's arm, forcing him to release. Leo's arrow slipped right through one of the creatures like a cloud. Caden pushed Leo and Emer deeper into the cave, swearing again.

"Devils, we're so dead. Keep moving, we need to lose them in these tunnels."

"Even if we lose ourselves?" Marin whispered back.

Emer uncoiled another round from the vine phone. "We can follow the vine back to the entrance."

"Wise," Ranae said, "but what keeps them from using it to follow us? This is foolish. We do not even know what chases us."

"Nightmares," Caden said, pushing everyone to move deeper into the cave. They didn't take the first tunnel to break off, but the third. They continued down the new tunnel until the entry was out of sight. Only then, did Caden let them stop.

Leo grunted, "What's to stop them from sniffing us out?"

Caden didn't have an answer, so Emer made one for him. "I can grow some fragrant plants to disguise our scents."

"Great," Caden said. "Why hadn't we done that when running into the Midnight Forest?"

"Sometimes smart ideas only come after mistakes made in desperation."

Emer started whispering mold and mosses into bloom while Caden grumbled, "And what we're doing now is as stupid as desperation goes. Put out that light," he hissed. Pearl yelped and extinguished the small ball of magical light in her hand.

Leo growled, "Caden, what's—"

"Shh!"

No one else attempted to argue as the disturbed cries echoed into the cave. Pungent smells of wet moss filled the air around them. Emer hoped the smell and dark was enough to hide her and her friends. Everyone held their breath, waiting to hear if the agitated horse-sounds grew closer. After a few minutes, the sounds faded, but no one dared to move for another minute following.

Caden released a heavy breath of relief. "I think we've lost them."

"How?" Leo asked. "They saw us hide in here."

"What were those things?" Emer asked.

Pearl ignited another small ball of light, just enough to see the contours of their faces.

Caden met Emer's eyes, but hesitated. Was it because he was still catching his breath or because he feared to even speak of the creatures?

"They're the mære—the spawn of nightmares," he said.

"Shrooms," Mica cursed. "I thought so, but—oh, shrooms, how are we still alive? I thought they only left survivors in nightmares."

Leo scoffed. "They weren't mære. Mære are just bedtime stories."

"Then what else were those things?" Caden asked. "What else fits the description of black scaled two-legged horses with fish tails? What else can make ogres run with fear? What else can outrun them and move like smoke? What else can destroy an entire battalion of ogres that easily?"

"Pardon me," Pearl peeped. "I have never heard of a mære. If they saved us from the ogres, is it possible they mean to aid us?"

"No!"

Emer jumped as the same resounding answer came from Caden, Mica, and Leo.

When the echoes of their negative statement faded, Caden said, "The only way we know about them is through the prophetess."

"And the scary stories," Mica added.

Leo huffed. "None of those are real."

"They are too," Mica argued. "My grandpa's cousin once saw one. He said they could turn into smoke, and no weapon of man or divinity could hurt—"

"That's foolishness," Leo said. "If we believe every story from every nut job about those creatures, they'd be immortal."

Caden grunted. "But your arrow slipped right through one without a scratch."

"Please explain," Marin said. "Do you have information about these creatures or not?"

"No," Leo said while Mica said, "We have lots of stories," and Caden said, "A little."

Emer gestured to Caden. "I trust Caden's research. He sifted through prophesies and legends to find us. You were the first to recognize the creatures. What do you know about them?"

He raised his hand to rub the back of his neck. "Not a lot. There's no record of them until the prophetess of Rezhina. She foretold the destruction of Veriae by 'creatures from the depths, who walked as men, but swam as fish, and ran as horses.'"

"Back up," Ranae said. "Veriae was destroyed? Those creatures single-handedly dismantled the capital of Ormio?"

Caden took a deep breath before continuing. "There aren't any reliable accounts from those who claimed to survive the attack. However, there are verified reports from people who visited the city after. A large part of the northern section was flooded. Another section to the west was burnt to the ground. Many buildings on the southern part of the city were blown over. It's as if the city was hit by a variety of natural disasters…but the bodies said it was anything but natural. The bodies that hadn't been lost in the sea, burnt to a crisp, or buried by buildings had been… mauled."

"Then," Marin said, "no one truly knows what happened?"

"No," Caden said. "But there were sightings. Nothing verifiable, but enough to spread rumors about nightmare-ish mares from—well, from the mare. Hence their name, mære."

Marin frowned. "Then those are the monsters that made the merpeople in Denebrae leave the lake?"

"It's a safe assumption," Caden said. "The prophetess warned again that the curse of Veriae would strike any who sailed the Imazhin. 'Land is your refuge.'"

Emer took a turn to question Caden. "But you were planning to sail to Noz Isle?"

"Yes," he said, rubbing the back of his neck. "I didn't know the mære were real. As Princess Aquamarine pointed out, there wasn't any verifiable proof that the mære destroyed the city or that they even existed. There haven't been any verifiable sightings in decades."

Mica shuffled closer to Pearl. "It was something I considered when accepting the plan to search for the sleeping princesses rather than cross the lake to petition the false queen."

"Then why now?" Emer asked. "Why did they target us?"

Caden shrugged. "I wish I knew."

Chapter 14

EMER

There was no use waiting until night to cross the bridge into Ormio. According to Caden's research, the mære were equally active at night as they haunted dreams. Emer and her friends waited until sunset in the Ezuthithe Cave tunnels before turning around the bend to the main tunnel and emerging quietly.

Their horses and carriage were gone, scared off by the mære and unable to enter the caves' narrow and jagged tunnels. Leo swore under his breath, but the group didn't need his tracking skills to follow the path of the spooked horses with the carriage. They found the horses and badly damaged carriage a couple of kilometers away. One of the front wheels had come unhinged. They camped there for the night as Emer encouraged a tree branch to grow in the appropriate shapes to replace the missing spokes before Ranae chopped them off and made the repairs.

Caden spent the entire evening apologizing and babying his horse. "Tucker's a proud breed," Caden defended against the eyebrow raises. "He won't let me mount him again until he knows I'm sorry. Which I am," he said, turning back to the animal.

They returned to the bridge the next morning, walking quietly, speaking only in whispers. They were too frightened of the mære's return and too somber from the massacre on the riverbank.

No more than fifty meters from the bridge, the entire ogre battalion lay to waste. The wretched smell of blood blew in the wind. There wasn't a single black-scaled body among the dead.

The mære had defeated all those ogres without a single casualty on their side? Emer's heart tightened with the thought.

"Should we search for survivors?" Pearl asked.

Leo grunted. "Only to end their misery and make sure they don't come after us again."

Pearl whimpered at his harshness, though Caden sighed to agree.

"Maybe someday," he said, "I'll feel sadness instead of relief over an ogre's death, but not today. Not for the past five years of war. We might find some useful information from one of them—"

"We don't have time," Leo said. "Ruby and Dot are waiting."

"Right." Caden nodded then led them across the bridge and into Ormio.

The Ormytha forest always surprised Emer. It wasn't full of green trees with spiked needles like the forests of Sophor or Midnight in Somnus. Its trees had white trunks with wide and flat leaves that changed colors in the autumn. Even now, they displayed beautiful colors of red, orange, and yellow. They broke away from their branches and drifted like little boats in the wind, carpeting the dirt road. The smell of ogre blood became replaced by the smell of decaying leaves. Emer shivered as she considered the death they left behind and the death that now surrounded them.

After a few minutes and several meters between them and the lake, Leo asked loudly, "Where are we going?"

"To find Princesses Ruby and Peridot," Caden said. "Did you forget?"

"No," the larger man growled. "But where are they exactly?"

Pearl answered, "Ruby and Dot were in Othium when Garnet left me with the dwarves. I believe they are somewhere in the forest."

Marin hummed a discouraged pitch. "Searching the entire Ormytha Forest would take months even if we split into groups."

"We aren't simply searching for a sleeping princess in the woods," Caden said. "Emer was surrounded by unnatural briar woods. You were surrounded by an unnatural whirlpool and Pearl by unnatural darkness. If we find a large unnatural phenomenon, we should find a sleeping princess in the center of it."

Leo growled. "That doesn't give us much to go on. It could still take us weeks to search every acre of these woods, not knowing what we're looking for."

"Hold on," Emer said. "I think I can help. Or, more accurately, I think I can ask the forest itself for help."

"How?" Leo asked.

Caden's smile grew into an amazed chuckle. "If you can do that, you're even more incredible than I thought."

Emer smirked back. "You thought I was anything less?"

"Not really. Give it a try."

She pinched back her smile as if that could hide her flattery. She wasn't sure she could use her connection to the plants to the extent she advertised, but now she had to try. Looking for the best way to connect to the forest, she found a tree with roots that arched out of the ground. She tapped Caden's shoulder to ask him to stop his horse, then dismounted.

"I know we need to hurry," she said. "Think of this as our trip to the docks to find Garnet's comb—"

"I'm going to stop you," Caden said, "if what you're doing now is as dangerous as that trip to the docks. You let go of the rope and swam around in that sleepy lake. With *mære*."

Emer frowned. "I only plan to talk with the trees. The risk is minimal."

"We thought the risk was minimal at the docks, but the more I learn about the lake, the worse it becomes!"

Emer spun on her heel to walk away. "Then stop learning more about the lake, because it turned out fine. This will only take ten minutes, but will hopefully save us weeks of searching."

"We trust you, Emer," Pearl said, cutting off Caden's next argument. "I will ponder on a way that I may ask Lucy to help us search for our friends."

Marin, however, turned her face away and slouched. "I will…also ponder on ways to be more helpful without abusing the environment with my magic."

Ranae gave her hand a comforting touch. "I think the environment is tougher than you believe. And you are too."

Emer smiled to agree, then went to the tree and sat between the roots. She pressed her back against the trunk and stroked her hands down the roots.

"Great trees of the Ormytha Forest," she whispered, closing her eyes. "Let me see through your leaves.

Connect me to your roots. Let me flow through you. Let me jump between your intertwining branches and entangled roots. You know there is something unnatural in this forest. Direct my mind to it. Show me what has disturbed the natural growth of this forest for these past hundred harvests."

As she spoke, she pictured the tree behind her, its rough bark scratching against her back, reaching upward to the sky, poking its leaves above the others to see the whole expanse of the forest to the foothills of the mountains. She felt its smooth roots digging into the ground and branching through the soil, weaving between the roots of the nearby shrubs and other trees. She grabbed onto the connection of the next tree, feeling her way through it as she had with the first. It was smaller, but had wider roots, reaching to a couple others. Emer felt guided to follow a specific path to a certain tree, then a bush, then another tree. She followed the path given to her, going away from the lake and toward the mountains.

Some of these trees were older than a hundred years. They remembered the days of Garnet traveling through them and returning with the Ormio twins. They felt the change that occurred when Ruby was put to sleep. New game paths were created, and certain plants no longer thrived in a specific area. A small glade became infested. The trees nearby became scratched and gnawed. Many others became posts for relieving—

Emer cringed and pulled herself from her meditation.

"South-west," she said, surprised to find Caden crouched in front of her. His hand rested on hers. She hadn't felt that while connected to the forest. Now, she rotated her hand to grasp his, relieved to sense his touch and unwilling to let go. It was no longer a simple desire that filled her concerning Caden. She needed him; his companionship, friendship, support, confidence in her…love for her. She needed him especially when she considered what she found in the forest.

"Ruby has nothing unnatural around her."

Unsure silence stiffened the air.

"Does that mean she's already awake?" Leo asked.

"Possibly," Emer said. "I sensed evidences of a highly active wolf pack staying around the area, but they have left."

"Wolves?" Marin shivered.

Mica blew out a puff of relieved breath. "If they left, then we don't need to fight our way through them."

"But why did they leave?" Leo growled. "Did she wake on her own? Did someone else wake her? She might be wandering around lost, and then Dot—"

"We'll find her," Caden said with calming re-assurance. His mouth pinched back a smile, hiding his amusement at Leo's reactions. Emer understood the expression as she mirrored it. The hunter prince was surprisingly passionate concerning the twins.

Emer led her friends south-west, touching a tree to check their path whenever they stopped to rest the horses.

After packing their midday meal and continuing their trek through the untraveled woods, Leo grunted and shifted his eyes northward. "Something's tracking us."

Caden frowned. "How can you tell?"

The large Braeder Prince grunted softly. "With my experience as a hunter, I can catch the signs of when I've become the hunted. Whatever's following us is stealthy, so it's not likely an ogre. Could it be a mære?" he asked Caden. "Do they hunt with stealth? Do they ever hunt solo, or are they purely pack hunters?"

Caden shook his head slowly. "I know too little about them to say either way. We saw them move and attack as a pack, but Emer and I saw one break from the pack to attack a single ogre."

"Actually," Mica added, "when they haunt people's dreams, it's one on one."

Caden muttered, "If the stories may be believed, yes. But the most verifiable sources only mention them attacking entire cities or boats, which suggests pack coordination."

Leo grunted, dissatisfied. "If it's not ogres or mære tracking us, then it's something else entirely, and I'm not sure if we can handle more enemies."

That wasn't encouraging. Emer wondered who else could be tracking them. The only other people they met were Hanzo, the citizens of Denebrae, and the odd couple who took Shinópu to Uldra. Who else would follow them? Could it be someone from their past? When Emer considered a third enemy, her mind went to her youngest sister. Was Queen Tanzanite following them through the woods? Emer had a hard time imagining the Queen of all Rezhina sneaking in the woods, but she also had a hard time imagining her youngest sister poisoning her and all the other princesses in the valley. If she was sneaky enough to poison all of them, perhaps she was sneaky enough to hunt them through the woods. Who knew how her sister had changed over the last hundred harvests—as if she'd known her well enough before.

The sun was well below the nearby mountain range before Leo let them stop for the night. Even still, he argued to stop only to stretch and rest the horses, then to continue through the night.

"Aren't you hungry?" Mica asked.

"I can eat while riding the coach." Leo scowled.

Marin set her hands on her hips, imitating the Somnus Queen. "The horses have traveled all day. It has been a long day for all of us, traveling through these rugged woods. We barely gave ourselves time to rest since leaving Denebrae, being chased by ogres and mære monsters."

Leo grunted with dissatisfaction, but dismounted the coach. "Maybe I shouldn't have given Shino my horse."

Caden frowned and asked, "Shino?"

"Er, yeah." The larger man shuffled. "He goes by a nickname in Texas. We're housemates on the farm."

Emer blinked wide eyes. "You dreamed of England again?"

"Not England," Leo said. "I know that much. It's another country called USA…but I forgot what it stood for."

"What interests me," Caden said, "is that your dreams include Shinópu, like Mica and I included each other."

Leo grunted, but Emer couldn't tell if that meant he didn't know or didn't want to tell them. He barely unpacked his bedding while everyone else worked on the fire and setting camp.

After eating, Pearl tried to reassure Leo with, "Rest now that your attitude may be bright when we find her on the morrow."

He grunted again and turned his back on her.

Emer wished it surprised her when she woke before dawn from a nightmare of mære and heard Caden's whispers. "Leo? Leeeooo?"

She sat up, blurry eyed and foggy minded. Shuffling on her boots, a kirtle, and travel cloak against the morning cold, she quietly closed the carriage door behind her. "Caden? What is it?"

"Emer?" Caden asked, surprised by her appearance. He seemed almost bashful at her messy morning hair. As if he hadn't woken her from sleeping before. "Sorry, did I wake you? You can go back to sleep."

"What is it?" Emer asked. "Is Leo in trouble?"

"I hope not," Caden said. "He took his things then abandoned us in the night. I'm sorry to wake you. Don't worry, I'll find him."

"Not likely," Emer said. "He probably went to find Ruby on his own. I can help you find him and keep you from becoming lost. Admit it, you need me."

He cringed. "You'd be safer staying in the coach, but I get the feeling that you won't accept no for an answer."

"That feeling would be correct," Emer said with a cheesy grin. "We can leave a note for the others when they wake."

He grunted, but relented.

While Caden scribbled a note, Emer touched a tree and connected with the forest again. It seemed Leo had moved slowly through the forest while tracking the old tracks of the wolves. He was less than a kilometer away from Ruby's cabin.

Emer shared this with Caden as he pulled her up to Tucker's saddle.

"Good," he said. "Even if the surrounding curse is gone, I don't think he should be alone."

"That," Emer teased, "and you want to witness history in the making when he finds her."

"That too," he admitted, then ordered his horse into a gallop.

Without a worn path and the need to keep pace with the others, Caden's horse showed off his true abilities for rugged travel. Tucker, it seemed, was incredibly agile, keeping their quick pace despite the uneven terrain. They leaped over bushes and boulders, weaving between trees like a sewing needle through fabric.

That explains Caden's loyalty to this prideful horse. Emer held on tightly to Caden, fearing the wild terrain and quick speed would buck her off. She asked them to slow as she grazed her hand down a tree branch. The weaving had turned them slightly eastward. She corrected Caden's direction, adding, "But the cabin is near. Leo just reached—"

She cut off as a shadow that was too human-like ducked behind a tree.

"Shield us!"

A thwick of a bow string was answered by a tree branch lowering to the exact angle. The tree cracked and splintered as it deflected a hunting arrow.

"Devils," Caden swore. "Who's after us this time?"

"Go!" Emer ducked herself into Caden's back as he hunched forward, urging Tucker faster.

"Hinder our pursuers," Emer said to the forest around them. "Clear our path to the cabin and show your strength against our unknown pursuer. Please? I know you can do this."

Even as she spoke, the foliage pulled away, creating a direct path to the cabin. She spotted the deserted and decaying little wooden home. How could it seem so close yet so far at the same time?

Caden straightened and chuckled with amazement. "Fine, you're right. I needed you to come with me."

Emer leaned to the right to tease him with a grin when a strange flower latched itself onto Caden's left shoulder. It burst with red petals and a large brown stem.

Caden yelled as the force kicked him forward.

"Caden!" Emer screamed, horrified by the arrow buried into his back shoulder. If she hadn't leaned over, it would have struck her instead. Guilt and worry clenched her heart as she considered how to help Caden and fight off their attacker. They needed help, but they were still a dozen meters from the cabin glade.

"Thank the devil it's my left arm," Caden growled.

"Caden?"

"The pain made me lose balance, but I can still ride. And all the more reason to."

Emer stared, amazed and terrified at the arrow sticking from both sides of his shoulder.

"You need a healer," she said.

"Later," he grunted, drawing his sword with his right arm.

They made it to the little cabin's glade, open enough to see the first sun rays breaking above the mountains. The bowman landed in a crouch directly to their left. Emer couldn't tell if he was a fully-grown man or a young man in the mid-stages of becoming a larger man. He wore a hooded patchwork of clothes with multiple layers dyed different shades of green and brown. His camouflaged outfit was specifically designed for blending and moving among forests.

Leo stepped out of the cabin, catching the mysterious attacker's attention. No. Leo did more than catch his attention. The attacker completely froze.

Caden used the distraction to aim a thrust at the man. He narrowly dodged, but Caden's sword caught on his hood.

Momentarily jolted from the capture between fabric, Caden yanked his sword free from the hood, slicing the fabric and letting it fall from the attacker's face.

Their attacker was younger than Emer expected. He had the face of a youth, maybe a year younger than herself.

Leo took his turn to become still as stone.

"Chase?" Leo whispered.

The young mysterious attacker grabbed what remained of his hood and pulled it over his face. Then, as quickly as he came, he ran away, leaping between trees and bounding over bushes out of sight.

With the threat gone, Emer turned to Leo for answers. "Ruby," she asked, "is she—"

"She's inside," Leo said, his voice scratchy. "We were too late."

Chapter 15

EMER

One look was all it took. Ruby wasn't simply sleeping on the bed. Her eyelids didn't flutter with dreams. Her abdomen didn't rise and fall with slow breaths. She didn't move at all.

"No!" Emer cried, turning away, unable to bear the sight. Caden wrapped his unwounded arm around her as if he could shelter her from the truth. No hug would blot out the stain in Emer's mind—the one look.

When she braved to look again—surely she was mistaken—Leo was stepping closer, reaching as if to capture a dream. He breathed heavily, sniffled and blinked hard.

"Leo," Caden said, "you don't have to be here—"

"We were too late," he croaked. "Somehow, I knew we would be. After she… After my first dream…I woke up with…dread."

"What do you mean?" Caden asked. Emer would thank him later for asking the questions that her heart was too broken to form. "You knew she'd be dead? What about Princess Peridot?"

"Dot," Leo said, gently scooping Ruby's hair to her right shoulder, "should be fine. For now. I think."

"That isn't reassuring, Leo."

"I know," he grunted. "We need to find her…but I can't leave Ruby like this."

Caden nodded. "She deserves the services of a princess. Do we have time for a funeral?"

"We must," Emer said, finally finding her voice. "As soon as the others arrive. In the meantime, you need that arrow removed. A funeral for one is bad enough."

Caden winced and gestured for Leo to join them outside. "Can I get some help? He kind of shot me."

"Kind of?" Emer repeated, incredulous.

"Better me than you," he said, touching her shoulder. "My pain would be the same if you were shot instead."

Leo seemed glad for the distraction as he immediately set about with rudimentary first aid. Caden sat and leaned his un-arrowed shoulder against the cabin wall for the procedure.

Unable to handle Caden's shouts of pain and the returning image of Ruby's body, Emer spoke to the forest, asking it to clear a direct path to her sisters. The sooner they came, the sooner they could leave the awful place. With the path made and Caden's agony tapered, she returned to the men by the cabin.

"Here, let me help you with that bandage."

Caden winced around a smirk. "It's just a flesh wound."

Emer pouted. "I remember you saying that in England, as if it was a joke. Am I missing something?"

"Wait," Leo paused to frown as he applied a heavy helping of healing moss to Caden's front wound. "Was that a quote from *Monty Python and the Holy Grail*?"

Caden's eyebrows went high. "You know it?"

Leo shook his head, confused. "I don't dream of England, but I know that story. It's a—what do they call it—cult classic? Beshrews, was I part of a cult?"

The more they said, the more confused Emer became. How could they joke so close to tragedy? Their regular glances in Ruby's direction said they hadn't forgotten about her. Maybe it was because of the tragedy, they needed something—anything—to distract them.

Leo was nearly finished with Caden's wrap when the bandaged man said, "Speaking of King Arthur and backstabbing best friends, you recognized the bowman."

Leo stared at the trees as if he expected the young attacker to return. "I don't know. I thought I did."

What a confusing answer.

Caden groaned and rolled to sit with his back against the cabin.

"Who was he?" Emer asked. "He seemed to recognize you too."

The hunter swallowed, then finally managed to pull his attention away from the last known sighting of the young attacker.

"If he's the man I think he is, his name is Chase Bahr, Prince of Braeder. He is my younger brother."

"I didn't know you had a brother," Caden said.

Leo shook his head slowly. "I haven't for many years. I hardly recognized him, but he has Mother's face."

"How do you go years without seeing your brother?" Emer asked.

Caden smirked and nudged her. "You went a full century without seeing your sisters."

"I was asleep—" she nudged him back "—and that time passed to me in a matter of weeks. What was your excuse, Leo?"

"I thought he was dead," Leo said. "The ogre king said that if my parents plotted against them in any way, they would kill us, starting with my brother. My parents were never the type to follow someone else's rules, and Chase was brave. He was willing to risk his own life for the possibility of overthrowing the ogres. But they discovered his plots. They took him away from us in the middle of dinner. I never saw him again. I never thought I would."

"How long ago was that?"

"That was near the beginning of Braeder's downfall, three years ago. He was so young and stubborn back then. He should be on the brink of manhood now. It makes sense that he's the third party who was tracking us. Despite his youth, he was always skilled at the hunt. The question is why is he hunting us?"

"There you are!" a voice shrilled from the forest. Marin almost jumped off of Ranae's horse in her eagerness to join Emer at the cabin. "Is Ruby inside?"

Emer cringed. "Yes, and there she will remain. We were too late."

"Wha-what do you mean, 'too late?'" Pearl asked from Mica's horse. Her pale face became impossibly more pale.

Emer lost the heart to deliver the news, but thankfully, Caden jumped in to explain, "We didn't wake her in time. Leo suspects she died about the time of his first dream."

Any more words from Pearl became choked by her tears. Marin bowed her head solemnly.

Hoping to help her sisters, Emer found her voice again. "She deserves a burial. We may not have time to gather enough people to prove her importance, but, if I recall, Ormio put more prestige in the words accompanying the funeral than the people."

"Yes," Ranae said. "While Somnus religions focused on the Goddesses, Ormio focused on their words. The way to honor an Ormio Princess in death is to leave as many words of praise around her."

Dismounting, he approached the cabin, then pulled out a knife. "Maybe we can carve words into the cabin walls to mark her burial?"

"A fine idea," Marin said, joining his side, "though perhaps someone practiced in lettering shall do the carving."

He smirked and handed her the knife. Leo passed out extra knives as each of them took a section of the cabin to carve a few words into the walls. Over the door, Marin carved, "Here lies Princess Ruby of Ormio." They filled the walls with words like "Friend," "Sister," "Loved," and "Never to be forgotten."

Emer and her sisters shared stories of Ruby while they carved, talking about her enthusiasm to try any-thing as long as it was with her friends.

"She loved dogs," Pearl recalled, "as much as Dot loved birds. Do you remember when Ruby hid a burrowing pup in their shared bedchamber?"

212

Emer's smile cracked. "If I recall, Dot was going to tell on her until Ruby stole away one of the messenger birds for her."

Marin giggled. "I believe they were finally caught when their father heard the dog barking at the bird. Sometimes I wished to be as brazen as they were about their care for animals."

"Ruby's love for dogs might explain the wolves' presence," Caden said. "But what about their absence?"

Leo grunted. "After a quick survey of the grounds, it appears this place was crowded with dozens of wolves, maybe even a hundred based on the claw marks and game trails. Until recently. There's an elk carcass behind the cabin that's only a few days old. They might have known that Ruby was gone, and they abandoned their post."

"Where did they go?" Pearl asked, looking around like a spooked deer.

Leo grunted. Emer was unsure if the grunt meant "I don't know," or "I don't care." Maybe both?

Mica pointed at Caden's bandaged arm. "If the wolves were gone, what happened to you?"

"That's another story," Caden groaned, pausing to resituate his new arm sling. With urging from him and Emer, Leo shared with everyone about his long-lost brother. Caden had more questions, but the former Braeder Prince refused to answer.

After an hour, they stepped back to admire their handiwork on Ruby's final resting place.

"Now," Marin said, "to speak the words. May they continually echo within her walls and fill her soul with our love."

They each took turns to say the words and phrases they carved. "Determined." "Honest." "Bold." "Thoughtful."

While Emer had chosen words from her own experiences with Ruby, she was surprised by Caden's insightful research and Leo's personal touches. Instead of holding a feast around the grave as they did at Somnus funerals, they stepped silently away from the glade to let no other sounds disturb the echoes of their words.

Leo was the first to break the silence. "We can't lose Dot too."

"I agree," Caden said. "Emer, is it safe to ask the plants to navigate us to Princess Peridot?"

"I can ask," Emer said.

Finding a thicket of tall trees, she sat between two, resting her hands on their trunks.

"Great trees," she said, "thank you for helping us to find our friend. If I may, I plead with you again to guide me through your roots to another sister in trouble. She may be east of us and again surrounded by unnatural events. Please, direct me to her."

She pictured entering the tree trunks, flowing down into its roots, winding and crossing from plant to plant. She zipped back and forth, side to side, around and around until she broke the connection.

"I cannot get a heading," she said, disappointed. "They only took me in circles."

Again, Caden was kneeling beside her when she opened her eyes. Thankfully, his eyes spoke more of worry for her than disappointment in her abilities.

"Maybe she's not in the forest then," he said.

"Oh!" Pearl shouted with an idea. "Perhaps I can ask Lucy for help! Lucy, can you appear as a medium ball of light?" A ball as large as her head appeared before her.

Everyone else flinched and shielded their eyes from the light.

Ignoring the brightness, Pearl asked her ball of light, "Can you fly high in the air until your light lands on some odd phenomena such as a cloud of darkness, unnatural thicket of thorns, or gathering of wolves?"

The light floated into the air, rising higher and higher. Just when Emer thought she'd lose it in the daylight, it dropped back down.

"Lucy, if you may shrink to your candle-wick size and dim your light that we may see you—oh, thank you. Now, may you please spell out what you saw?"

The little light drew itself into lines, creating letters until it formed into the word, "Birds."

Emer blinked in surprise. While she felt emotions and impressions from her plants, Pearl's words of light were convenient.

"Birds?" Caden repeated. "In what direction?"

Pearl asked her light, and it created an arrow, pointing south-east.

Marin oriented herself by glancing at the mountains to the west. "I believe that leads us towards Othium."

"Ah." Caden nodded. "That would explain why Emer's plants couldn't find her. She's probably in the city."

Emer hoped he was right. They wouldn't know until they found her for sure. "Then onward we go."

Chapter 16

DOT

Irritation was a well-known companion who frequently met me through my twin sister. I was no stranger to the grinding teeth, rolling eyes, and heavy sighs. Every activity I began with Ruby started that way. No matter what I did, she wanted to do it too. No matter what I had, she wanted it too. It annoyed me beyond words that she found a way to do it even in my dreams. It made me want to scream along with the deafening pitch in my ears.

Yes, I was all too familiar with irritation. Anger, however, was new.

When I became bed-ridden and Ruby said Leo couldn't come visit me, I knew exactly what she was doing. I knew exactly why she was doing it. She wanted Leo for herself.

Why did she always end up with the things that were originally mine? What did she do to deserve them more than I did? What did she have that I didn't? Was it her redder hair?

What irritated me the most was my renewed desire for Leo. I wanted him more because Ruby wanted him. My strange ingrained love for him had started as confusion and curiosity, but after meeting him and seeing Ruby's connection with him, I found myself intrigued, flattered, then possessive. As if my feelings for Leo weren't complicated already, Ruby's involvement infuriated me.

The pain of my broken foot and the ever-present lump fed into my anger. My boredom didn't help. I missed the morning temple visits in Ormio, the meal planning with my sisters, then evening relaxations of drawing and practicing music. I even missed studying numbers and finances (Dia would have been proud of my longing).

Instead, I laid in bed all day with nothing to do but read, draw, stare out the window (hoping to see birds or Leo), and overthink everything. Lunch was my favorite time. Leo would sit on the porch with the best angle to my window and sign with me. He asked about my health, and comfort, and I asked about his job, adding a plea to ignore Ruby. From the beginning, she was far too friendly with him during lunches.

Mornings were my other favorite time as birds visited a feeder hanging from the porch covering. I'd watch them squabble over nuts and seeds, drawing a couple of them.

Between these small activities, I fell asleep and dreamed of Ormio and masquerades on Noz Isle. I preferred to sleep. Waking returned my consciousness to the lump beneath me and the deafening ringing in my ears. It was truly an injustice of the world that only roosters were allowed to wake up screaming.

Then, Ruby kissed Leo.

She had the audacity to do it in front of my window, keeping Leo's back to me so I could only guess the reasoning behind his uncomfortable body language.

I cried out as Leo pushed Ruby back. He spoke inaudible words before he turned to my window. His eyes went wide (with terror) when they met mine (with fury).

"This isn't real," he signed. "She kissed me without consent! I love *you*, Dot!"

At least one part was true: this wasn't real. This was a dream—an awful nightmare where my ears were screaming, my body was bruised and broken, and my heart was torn apart.

I pulled the curtains closed, too angry to see his face.

Before lunch the next day, I organized my fury into words and asked my mom to bring Ruby to me.

We did less talking than shouting, despite the speech-to-text. The only highlight of the whole conversation was when Ruby almost ran into the door on her way out. I wished she had.

The next days passed in silent solitude. I couldn't tell Mom what happened. She already disliked Leo and our too-young relationship. Calling him unfaithful (even if he had been unwilling) would only feed her argument.

I kept the curtains closed save for a small crack that let me see the bird feeder. I watched the local feather-friends in the mornings, filling my art pad with their images, wishing to join their flights home. Sometimes, I felt lonely enough to sign to them. Usually, movements scared birds, but perhaps they felt safe with the window barrier and were intrigued by my hand signs. (Maybe they sensed my loneliness?) Ruby sometimes talked about the emotional intelligence of dogs, but I was willing to argue that these dream birds were equally intelligent and understanding.

More birds visited me as the days went by, lingering longer at the feeder, sometimes hopping to my window sill to quirk their shiny little heads at me. I named a few that I recognized. I used names of my friends (I missed them so much) and non-present family members. The red robin that I named Garnet seemed to visit the most.

Five days after Ruby and Leo's kiss, I could hardly believe Ruby's audacity as she walked into the guest bedroom with my mom.

I shouted and nearly jumped from my bed. "Why's she here?" I signed to Mom. "I don't want to see her! Make her leave!"

"Dot," my mom signed, "calm down, why are you so angry at Biddy?"

Slanders, I couldn't tell my mom.

Angry beyond belief, I signed at Ruby with curt and jerky movements. "You pea-brain! I'll never forgive you!"

Mom frowned and signed with her own curtness, "Dot! I'm not translating that, be nice!"

I urged Mom to tell her anyway, but Mom's attention was back on Ruby's moving mouth. Of course. Always taking away the things that were mine.

Mom swallowed and fidgeted a bit more before responding. She turned back to me to translate, "Ruby says that she wants to talk to you, but she thinks you'll ignore her unless I'm here."

"She's right," I signed and moaned. "I don't want to talk with her or see her." (Or hear her screams in my head, for that matter.)

Mom scolded me again, but I gestured, adamant that she would speak my words.

Mom released a heavy breath then spoke to Ruby. My sister frowned and responded, despite my request for dismissal.

Mom translated, "Ruby says, 'I don't want to fight anymore. We're not waking up, so we should work together to make this our home now.'" Mom's eyebrows squished with confusion. Of course, she had no idea that we were dreaming. I was too angry to worry over talking about Ormio in front of Mom.

"This isn't home!" I signed. "Why have you given up on returning home? Everything can go back to normal if we wake up."

Mom's squished eyebrows became even more wrinkly. She asked, "What do you mean?"

I simply pointed at Ruby as her mouth moved. She pursed her lips and wiggled her head with undeniable sass.

Mom translated, "All you think about is leaving, but I want to stay. That's why I'd be better for Leo. The dumb man doesn't know what's good for him."

"Lies!" I signed. "He's not dumb! I don't want to leave Leo—I care about him, and I know I'll miss him, but this is a dream! This isn't real, and I'm miserable here! The new bird species and Leo's affections are the only good parts, but he loves Dorothy, not me."

Mom got halfway through my words before she clamped her mouth shut and folded her arms.

"Mom!" I signed. Ruby mouthed the word too, earning a sharp and slightly terrified stare from the queen look-alike.

Speaking and signing, she said, "I'm not translating any more until you two explain what's going on here. You're fighting like sisters!"

"We *are* sisters!" I even used the clunky Signing Exact English to emphasize "are."

At the same time, Ruby said something that made Mom's face blanch with worried fear. I reached over and took my mom's hand. Signing with my freehand, I said, "You said it yourself, I changed after Leo left. You know I'm not Dorothy. I'm sorry, I don't know what happened to her or why I have her memories, but I don't belong here."

Mom did nothing to reply, but her heavy swallow and wide eyes spoke for her. She knew I had changed. She knew her daughter, Dorothy, but I was different. Just as Ruby and I looked the same, we were different people.

Ruby continued rambling (spoiling all the secrets of Ormio, for all I knew), but Mom kept her eyes on me.

"I'm sorry," I signed, "but this is all a dream to me. In O-R-M-I-O, Ruby and I are twins. We have a brother and two more sisters. I miss them. I need to return to them."

Mom raised her hands around her head as she shook it, as if our words were insane. I couldn't blame her. She dashed out of the room, leaving me alone with Ruby. My twin must have heard Mom's departure as she pulled out her phone and text-to-speech app. She showed me the screen and her written words.

"Well, that could have gone better."

"No kidding," I typed back and pushed the button to read it aloud.

Ruby replied, "Do you really want to wake up and leave? This world is broken, and we could fix it."

I shook my head as if she could see me. "Ormio's also broken. Or did you forget about the war with Huiess and Tanzi going crazy?"

Ruby shrugged. "Even as princesses, we couldn't do anything about those problems. But Mom and Dad—if they can be together, then this world will be…much nicer."

I scoffed. Maybe for her, but she wasn't stuck in bed.

Ruby left, and I pulled out my art pad. I spent the evening drawing Mom as the woman I remembered; the Queen of Ormio. Next, I drew Dia with her ledgers, Cephas with his rock collection, and Opal with her lucky jewelry. I must have fallen asleep with my pad still open as I woke to find Mom flipping through the pages and my dinner tray set aside. Her little frown and raised eyebrows looked both impressed and uneasy.

Noticing me, she asked, "When did you draw these?"

"Before my nap," I signed.

She nodded and pointed to the pictures of my siblings. "Who are they?"

I cringed. My mom didn't recognize my siblings—her own children in another world. Even if she didn't believe me, I wanted to remedy that problem. I talked about each of my siblings in detail, almost enjoying the sense of longing in my heart that came with the discussion.

My mom listened, but her little frown didn't go away. She flipped to an earlier drawing, one of Leo sitting on the porch bench during lunch, smiling at me through the window. I'd even managed to capture the tenderness in his eyes.

"What about him?" Mom asked.

I shook my head. "I didn't know him until I came here. I only have Dorothy's memories of him. But that's enough to tell me that he's a good man." (Despite Ruby's advances on him.) "That's why I wanted to see him so badly." Even still, I sensed that he held the secret to wake me from this awful dream. The thought of asking him to help me wake up made me both anxious to wake and also sad to leave him.

Mom shook her head, confused. "Whatever's happening, I hope you figure it out soon. Just remember; I'll always love you, Dot, no matter who you decide to be, what you do, or where you go."

Chapter 17

RUBY

I felt a little better after my conversation with Dot that didn't end with a slammed door. I tried smoothing things over with Leo, but one week after kissing him, he still acted awkward. I felt dead inside, unable to make him like me, unwilling to admit to Dot that she won. Even the darkness of my vision seemed colder and more like empty space than the confines of a wolf's stomach. My only success or happiness came from my sneaky attempts to put my mom and dad together.

Mom acted a little awkward around me, like she'd rather ignore me than ask me to explain how Dot and I were sisters. She would have known if she'd given birth to twins.

During lunches, I purposefully left my usual spot open next to Dad. More often than not, Mom took it. The rearrangements of seats sometimes put Leo or Shino next to me. Both were mostly silent, but Leo's coldness toward me was almost tangible. Dad even mentioned Leo's chilled attitude affecting his work, telling Mom one afternoon in the living room, "I'd hate to send you two away, but I think Dot's presence is souring Leo's work ethics. No one wants to work around him because he's such a miserable grump."

"Dot's been a bit miserable too. Thank you for your hospitality, but it might be better for us to leave tomorrow."

Slanders, I couldn't let Mom leave. Dad hadn't taken her on a proper outing yet. I had to talk to Leo.

Calling for Rayban, I snuck out of the house and followed my dog's lead to Leo's cottage.

Before I reached his home, a gruff voice grumbled, "What are you doing here, Ruby?"

Leo.

Why did my heart clench every time I heard his voice? Before, his voice made my heart tense with nerves and excitement. Now, it tensed with unease and physical pain.

Forcing myself to speak, I said, "I came to talk."

He groaned. "Leave me alone." His heavy footsteps turned away.

His voice was like the tip of a blade poking through a bag. The weight of the contents ripped the pinprick into a giant hole for everything to spill out.

228

"Please, Leo," I begged, and Leo's footsteps paused. "You're the only one who could possibly understand. Dot and I are dreaming—you heard her confirm it! The Dot you knew is gone and switched by my sister. She doesn't know you like I do. She doesn't want to stay here with you…like I do."

The dirt scrunched beneath his feet as he turned sharply on me. He growled, "Don't put words in her mouth! Of course, you didn't see us signing to each other through the window during lunch. Our love is stronger than any barrier you put between us."

They'd been signing to each other during lunches? Having secret conversations without me knowing. Without me seeing.

Despite everything I tried, all I did was drive Leo farther away from me.

"I'm sorry," I burst. "I didn't mean to ruin your relationship with Dot. Er—no, that's a lie. I did. But I didn't mean to make you miserable."

He said nothing.

"But I see now—or, at least, I understand now. And I'm sorry. I'll stop trying. I'll give up on you."

I hoped that he'd tell me to never give up, to never stop trying.

Instead, he grunted.

What did he mean by that? I asked, "Does that mean you forgive me?"

"It means I can't wait for this summer to be over."

Slanders, I really had made him miserable. He wouldn't give me the satisfaction of forgiveness because he didn't want to. He wanted to leave me and return to his home in Washington with Dot, to forget about me and pretend it never happened.

My eyes and nose burned as tears threatened to expose my feelings. "I'll fix it," I said. "I'm helping my mom and dad fall for each other. I'll help you and Dot too."

"Don't," Leo said. "I don't need you messing with my life any more than you already have. Just leave me alone."

He stomped off to his residence, slamming the door closed. I dug my heels into the ground. Why wouldn't he let me try to fix it?

The tears from before made good on their threats as my frustration, rejection, and broken heart tore me apart. I knelt to the ground and sobbed. Rayban whined and licked my salted face. I wrapped my arms around him and buried my tears into his fur. He twisted around, continuing to lick my arm and face—wherever he could reach. Would those be the most loving kisses I ever received? Why couldn't a man love me as easily as Rayban did?

"Miss Fashingbauer?"

I barely heard Shino's quiet voice between my cries.

"What hurts?"

"Everything," I moaned, sliding my face out of Rayban's fur and loosening my hug.

"Should I call a doctor?"

"No. He can't fix this."

"I will run for Mr. Fashingbauer."

"No, don't leave," I said, reaching for him. As much as I appreciated Rayban's comfort, I needed someone to talk to, someone who'd talk back. I needed someone to argue with the voices in my head that said I was an unwanted failure. Normally, I talked to my sisters about my troubles. Dot was usually the cause for them—as she was now—but Opal and Dia hadn't joined this confusing dream. I wanted to talk it over with my dad, but he'd probably send Leo packing if he knew everything. Then Mom and Dot would follow.

"Are you still there?" I asked Shino. He was so quiet.

"Yes," he said. Based on the location of his voice, he hadn't moved.

"Will you sit with me?"

I barely heard the rustle of his clothes as he sat on the ground beside me.

"Is this good?"

"Better," I said, but was still unsatisfied. He was too quiet. He could disappear without my notice, but I didn't want to be left alone. I slid closer until I felt his arm against mine. I grabbed his wrist and cried into his shoulder.

He stiffened from the contact, but after a good minute, he relaxed and asked, "Who needs punishment?"

"What?"

"Who caused the tears?"

"Oh." I sniffled and wiped my useless eyes. "I did. And Leo and Dot, sort of. No matter what I do, where I go, or where she is, Dot always gets the things I want."

"What things?" he asked.

Leo. Instead, I said, "Something I can't have."

Shino chuckled and murmured something in his native language.

"What was that?" I asked.

"A saying," he said, his voice small. He explained, "Ah, it says…The winds of tomorrow will blow tomorrow."

After a moment of pondering, I gave up. "I don't get it."

"Ah, maybe it means something different in English. It means not to worry about bad days. Tomorrow is a new day."

"The winds of tomorrow will blow tomorrow," I repeated. It was a nice thought. "Do you have any other insightful sayings?"

He chuckled with an edge of nerves. "Many."

"Do you have a favorite?"

He spoke a long phrase that was somehow both strange and beautiful at the same time. "What does it mean?" I asked.

"Even, ah, what is the word for dirt on shelves?"

"Dust?"

"Dust," he repeated as if it was the most important word of the day. "The saying is, 'Even dust, when piled, can become a mountain.'"

"Huh." I smirked as I considered it. "Like, don't discount the little things?'"

He vocalized his nod with a simple, "Hmm. Every part is important."

I pondered on that, wondering about the little parts I made these past few weeks of being a Texan. How big was my mountain, and what was I building?

I smiled and thanked him with a touch on the shoulder. "Thank you. And your English has gotten a lot better."

His hand touched mine, slow and timid, like he wasn't sure if it was the right thing to do. My smile broadened. Who could frown around such adorable innocence?

No, I wasn't allowed to be happy when Leo was miserable. Even if Shino…Slanders, was he flirting with me?

He said another long phrase from his native tongue.

"What was that?"

"Thanks for talking with heart."

I pulled my hand away from his shoulder, tingling from the lines drawn by his fingers as my hand slid from underneath his.

Whispering, terrified of the answer, I asked, "What do you want, Shino?"

"Ah, how to say it? They say that Americans like to be bold."

"Stop," I said, holding up my hand. If he confessed feelings for me, I'd break his heart as Leo had broken mine. Awkward as the moment was, I couldn't put someone else through the same pain I suffered. "Shino, one day, you'll make someone very happy."

Shino gave a confused grunt to vocalize his frown.

"But not me," I said, standing. "Not today. Excuse me."

I promptly turned and hastened toward the house, asking Rayban for correct directions after several paces. My confused whirlwind of thoughts screeched to a halt as I heard Mom talking to Dot about packing.

No. Not yet. I still needed to fix everything!

"Dad?" I called. He responded with a shout back from his bedroom. Feeling the walls to him, I stepped in and decided there wasn't time to be subtle.

"Dad? I don't want Candi and Dot to leave."

"Biddy—"

"Leo's miserable because he hasn't been able to see Dot. If Leo sees Dot on a regular basis, I bet his mood and work will improve."

"I've never let the field workers inside the house—partially for your protection."

"Trust me, Leo's not interested in me. Also, me or Mo—uh, Candi can supervise. We three women can overpower him, blindness and deafness notwithstanding."

Dad chuckled a little at that thought.

"Please," I begged. "Let them stay. Don't you want Candi to stay?"

For some reason, that made my dad sing, "I want candy."

"Um, wow, I didn't expect a confession."

"It's a song, Biddy!" he blustered and laughed. "You know, by The Strangeloves."

"The who?"

"No, no. The Who is a different group—same decade though."

Usually this dream state filled my culture gaps with memories, but I was left blank this time. "What are you talking about?"

He simply laughed harder. "Nevermind. I can talk to Candi and ask them if they're comfortable with visits from Leo."

"Excellent, I'll go tell Leo!"

"Biddy, hold on. Are you sure about this? Will you be comfortable with Leo coming through the house?"

Did Dad know of my kiss attempt? Either way, I was determined to fix every broken heart on this property. Pretending it didn't matter to me, I said, "If he tries anything improper, I can sic Rayban on him."

As much as I wanted to share the news with Leo, I waited to make sure Dad talked with Mom and Dot first. They discussed and negotiated terms for Leo to come into the house and see Dot. My sister seemed reluctant and almost nervous, but hoped to see him at least once before leaving.

By the time they decided on all the particulars, the night was too late to tell Leo the good news. I enjoyed a good dinner and breakfast before asking Rayban to direct me to his cottage. Since it was the weekend, the workers had the day off to enjoy however they wanted, meaning they'd be home in the mid-morning.

Rayban and I went to Leo and Shino's home, feeling the doorways to count my way to theirs. I knocked and waited. They were inside. The shuffling and grunts behind the door confirmed it. The cottage was small enough that even if they both stood on the opposite side, it wouldn't take more than a few seconds to open the door. Yet I waited. I knocked again and waited longer.

After a painful sixteen seconds, the door opened.

"Hello, Ms. Fashingbauer," Shino said.

Filling my stomach twice since Leo's bitterness helped reorient my heart, which did a funny flip-flop with happiness and disappointment. While I was happy to hear from Shino, I hadn't come to speak with him, which turned the whole flip and flop into an awkward tumble as I said, "Hey, Shino. Can I talk to Leo?"

"Oh." I could almost hear his mood dampen as guilt slapped my heart like a wet rag. "Le—ah, he does not want to talk."

What was I—the cart for all disappointments? Pile it on, everyone!

"Well," I said, "I made arrangements for Leo to visit Dot during lunch breaks."

The door creaked as I supposed Leo and Shino shared a wordless exchange.

Then, a muttered, "Thanks," came from deeper within the cottage.

Shino cleared his throat and asked, "Can we talk outside?"

I nodded and stepped back, assuming he needed space to exit his home. My heel met the edge of their porch. My arms swung madly for balance and Rayban barked. The porch was only a single step off the ground, but fear shot through me as I fell backward.

A hand caught my arm and pulled me up. My hands reached for something stable and found Shino's chest.

"Ms. Fashingbauer?" he asked, holding me upright.

"Shino," I gasped. "After saving me, I think you've earned the right to call me Biddy."

He chuckled nervously and tested my balance before fully releasing me. I immediately missed his touch. With my feet solidly on the ground and Rayban nudging me away from the porch edge, I asked, "What did you want to talk about?"

"Do the winds of tomorrow blow tomorrow?"

"Am I doing better today?" I clarified. "Healing takes time. I still feel like a tractor ran over my chest… But I guess I'm a little better. Your words helped."

He grunted. I wanted him to ask me more, but he returned to silence. Perhaps he was also still stung from me cutting off his feelings.

"Shino," I asked, "if you liked me, but someone else liked me too, would you fight for me?"

"I would fight to the death to protect what is mine." My heart lifted off the ground, but before it could take off, he continued, "But I do not chase things that belong to others."

His words weighed heavy with meaning. He didn't see me as his own. He knew I'd given my heart to Leo. But it wasn't Leo's. Not entirely. Not anymore.

"What if," I said, "it was half yours?"

"A divided heart will always be broken."

Ouch. Profound, but ouch.

I nodded, annoyed, but unable to deny the truth. "Well, as I said, healing takes time. I'll see you around." Satisfied that my message had been received, I asked Rayban to lead me home.

Chapter 18

SHINÓPU

Uldra had never been a place where dreams came true. Not for Shinópu. He remembered the first time he entered the great capital city of Veenigz with a battalion of ogres, heading a procession for the king and queen and their spoiled daughter, Charlotte. After five years of being an enslaved guard for the royal ogres, Shinópu was familiar with the chaos that greeted them in Veenigz. It was the last stronghold in the grasslands against ogres, backed against the wall of the southern Rezhina Mountain Range.

There had been little space to walk as trampled tents were strewn across the streets in front of pillaged buildings. The city was overcrowded with defeated refugees from Zubra and even Braeder.

Shinópu hadn't seen any dwarves from Chafan.

He had thought the city was hideous. Why would anyone fight to stay in such a place?

Freedom had a way of opening one's eyes, to find goodness in life, and the reasons to fight to retain one's freedom.

Riding with unnatural speeds, he reached Uldra with Charger and Brooke in only nine days. As he stood at a doorway, staring at the city, he saw its beauty and worth. A blue river weaved between the buildings with white rooftops that blended into the Northern cliffs of the Rezhina Mountains. Thin waterfalls streamed down the great cliffs, adding glistening stripes to the white horizon. Built into the cliffs as the city centerpiece was a castle grand enough to be called a palace. Its flat walls and many turrets made the castle nearly impenetrable.

Yet, there he was, about to storm it.

Shinópu had never been in an army. He'd been trained to fight in regulated duels as the prince of Chafan. However, ogres didn't fight with regulations and rules. Shinópu had been captured as a youth, then enslaved when the ogres recognized his dual sword wielding talent. They drafted him as a guard for the royal family. He'd tried a couple of times to attack them. The other guards quickly put a stop to his attempts, and the punishments were severe.

Now, he didn't simply join an army. He led it. He knew how ogres attacked. He knew how they rested by plundering and holing away until they grew bored and eager to fight again.

He also knew his men—no, his dwarves—his people. He knew their patience as they waited and trained the last half-decade in the caverns. He knew their loyalty and high regard for honor. They would do what they believed to be right, even if it killed them.

Not unlike the family of his dream from the previous nights.

Shinópu allowed his mind to wander as he reflected on his recent dreams. He worked on a cotton farm beside Leo. He worked an honest day, then his favorite part was grabbing lunch, where he'd spot the landowner's daughter, Ruby. Even after a hard morning of sweating in the sun, her smile would lighten his mood and brighten his day. Her red hair reminded him of characters from unfamiliar stories. He admired her determination to be independent, despite her blindness. He liked her boldness and confidence. Maybe if he could be so bold, she would notice him more.

Were his dreams similar to those of Princes Seaver and Wright? If so, did that mean he should have stayed to help them wake Ruby?

Shinópu shook his head. He couldn't afford such thoughts. He had made his choice, and he would stick to it because people relied on him. He had come back to Uldra, and Charger took him directly to the dwarves. After five years of hiding and building their army, they'd resurfaced with the revolt in the castle. Unfortunately, ever since the revolt twelve days ago, the castle was occupied by an entire battalion of ogres and needed a purging. Shinópu would have been content as a swordsman, but Charger had revealed his identity. The dwarves still honored his family as their monarchy. Shinópu hadn't jumped at the idea of leading people he hadn't seen in years, but as soon as they discussed tactics, he realized the wealth of his knowledge from serving the royal ogre family.

One of his captains called his name and greeted him with a respectful nod. "The sun is almost set. We're ready."

Shinópu nodded and spoke in Dwarven, "Let's go."

He led his group of comrades back into the building, behind a bookshelf to a secret room, then under a rug to a secret tunnel. They walked quietly, sparing whispers when necessary.

It felt good to speak his native tongue again. He'd never really grasped the human language, filtering between the odd phrases and blending words to understand the ideas more than the exact meanings of what was said. He'd learned the subtle communication of inferences. The ogres had been easy to understand. With them, it was always "attack that," or "stay still."

There were also on-going orders to "Be silent," and "Stay out of my way."

The tunnel took Shinópu and his followers a couple of acres south-west before ending in a tailor shop. They crossed an alley to a storage house, winding around piles of forgotten junk until they came to a specific wooden box that covered another trap door. This tunnel had a few break offs, and they took the one that opened up at an abandoned school within a stone's throw of the castle.

More dwarves had joined them in the tunnels or waited for them in the school. There were only about fifty of them, but it was enough to separate into groups to perform their missions. Their main goal was to reach the dungeons where the regular castle guards were detained. Secondary goals included reclaiming the turrets for the high ground, protecting the King and Queen of Uldra, and securing the castle as a whole. The next step was to signal to those outside waiting to fall upon any fleeing ogres. They would purge the city of the ogre filth and reclaim the stronghold.

A cry sounded from the castle. Shinópu spied on the turrets as ogres gathered to the front, pointing at something in the distance. A line of fire grew somewhere at the edge of the city. Shinópu couldn't see it, but that was the plan—the distraction. He watched the ogres gather at the front, waiting for their attention to be wholly focused on the fires in the distance. With the distraction and the sun below the horizon, they'd be blind to the dwarves climbing the sides of the castle walls. He barely picked out their figures in the shadows, climbing over the walls and quietly removing the ogres from the turrets.

The captain stood beside Shinópu, waiting for his signal. He counted to ten, but it still seemed too early. He counted another five, then took a deep breath.

With a nod from Shinópu, the captain signaled someone on the roof to raise a simple green scarf into the air, attached to the end of a long pole. Dwarves raised the castle gates, and Shinópu charged for them with his little band. There was no battle cry, no inspiring speech. Just the rush of the run in the silence of the new night.

A skirmish broke out at the top of the barbican, but the gate remained open, and no bells sounded.

"Hurry," he hissed to his comrades, quickening their stride to run across the drawbridge.

The gate lowered a foot, but stopped with an ogreish cry. Shinópu winced at the sound piercing the night. He rushed under the gate and ran into a beefy ogre guard. He had likely come to inspect the noise. The ogre let out a single cry before Shinópu silenced him. His first blood for the night. He expected a lot more before the sun rose again.

His comrades took care of the other two guards who came to inspect the commotion as a warning bell echoed from above. It rang sooner than Shinópu planned, but at least his men were through the barbican and into the palace entry. They divided into their groups of ten to spread themselves through the halls. He'd have preferred larger groups, but speed was their prerogative, and larger groups were less effective in the castle corridors.

Hoping their intel was still accurate, Shinópu led his comrades up the stairs. They met and quickly dealt with two more ogres. Despite the gore and terror of the battle, Shinópu congratulated his comrades.

"That was a good fight, with honor."

Before they could honor him back, he continued their dash down the hallway. Across a courtyard corridor and down another hallway, they fought several more ogres before breaching a guarded door. His comrades were growing tired, and the ogres were converging on them.

With no time to waste, Shinópu barged through the door.

"Men of Uldra!" he shouted into the room. "Rise and fight!"

The guards inside wore tattered green and white tabards with dragon crests. They must have heard the bells of battle, because several of them were already standing and prepared to fight with their fists.

That was unnecessary.

Shinópu tossed some recently won ogre-swords at their feet. The men grinned, picked up the weapons, then spilled out of the room. They roared with battle cries as they raised their swords and charged at the oncoming ogres.

They fought their way through the castle to the king and queen's room. Shinópu sighed with relief to find that the company sent to secure them had successfully distracted the ogre king and queen with a heated argument. Knowing their temperaments, Shinópu had suggested the tactic to disarm them.

They ran into fewer ogres as they continued through the corridors. Crossing a courtyard, Shinópu spotted the highest turret.

They'd raised the Uldra flag with a top grassy green half, bottom rocky white half, and a gold river line between. It was more than a symbol of their land. It was a symbol of their independence and freedom.

Dwarves and men cheered and hollered with victory. They had a long way to go before Uldra was completely free, but recapturing the castle was a tipping point in their favor.

They'd pushed the remaining ogres back into the city, where they'd met the larger battalion of dwarves.

Shinópu grinned and led the charge beside the castle's captain of the guard. With the castle secured, they pushed their way to the city, dividing and spreading themselves through the narrow alleys like the fingers of a river pushing into the ocean. After many divisions, Shinópu chased the ogres with his group of ten comrades, fellow dwarves whom he'd quickly come to trust. They fought any ogre in sight until the monsters began to flee before them. With the line of fire surrounding half of the city's north side, the ogres were funneled to the sides where the remains of the human army waited.

It was a gentle race to steer them until more ogre roars sounded behind Shinópu's group.

"How did they get behind us?" a comrade asked.

"Doesn't matter," Shinópu growled. "Lead them to the humans then duck into a building."

"And what if the ogres ahead decide to turn back on us?"

Shinópu grunted without an answer.

The ogres ahead slowed as they funneled across the river bridge. Shinópu's group didn't need to engage in battle with them, simply herd them toward the humans…but they couldn't be caught by the group behind.

They began to follow the ogres across the bridge, when they turned around. Shinópu stopped in the middle of the bridge, blocked in by ogres at both ends.

"Push the group ahead," Shinópu said. "I'll stop the group behind from following."

"Prince—"

"That was an order!"

His captain saluted him, then put his back to Shinópu's to chase the ogres ahead.

Shinópu stared down the ogre group from behind and brandished his swords. Being on the bridge meant that only three ogres could face him at once. He'd fought two at a time outside the Midnight Forest, but he doubted that he could do three.

They came. The bridge shook under their pounding charge. Shinópu released a slow breath before a quick intake and snapping into motion.

His swords weaved through bodies like a current. He was a fish cutting his way upriver, slipping through the gaps, pushing his way against the forces. He was no longer the terrified boy who watched as his parents were slaughtered. He was no longer the slave being ordered to kill others who didn't deserve death. He also wasn't an average and lonely swordsman. He was a freed dwarf. He was a leader and comrade— maybe even a friend to the other princes and princesses. He was the Prince of Chafan.

Pain erupted from his thigh as one of the ogres struck him. He stumbled and earned another slash of agony across his ribs. Someone screamed his name. A comrade? It had almost sounded like a young woman's cry.

His vision blurred and blackened. He hoped that Prince Seaver had found the other princesses. He would have liked to meet them. Instead, he fell to the stony bridge, pleased at least by the thought that his comrades had escaped. They'd still win the day, with or without him.

Chapter 19

EMER

Emer and her friends traveled for four days through Ormytha Forest before reaching the abandoned port city of Othium. They had taken a wider route off the forsaken path along the coast since their horses were too skittish to travel near the lake.

After their first full day of traveling, they spotted paw prints, tufts of fur, scratches in the trees, and gaming trails. They seemed to be following the wolf packs that left Ruby.

"Beshrews," Caden cursed. "If we're following the wolves, they're probably surrounding Princess Peridot now."

"In addition to the birds that Lucy spotted?" Pearl squeaked.

Leo frowned. "Is it because we were too late to save Ruby?"

"I don't know," Caden said, rubbing the back of his neck. "This hasn't happened before. Their surrounding curses always changed when they woke."

"Maybe," Emer tried, "being twins has something to do with it. If Leo dreamed of them together, perhaps they are sharing a dream like Marin and Ranae. Maybe they have similar powers."

Caden wrote down a couple of notes and nodded thoughtfully. "It's something to consider, but that doesn't solve the problem of how to pass them."

If only wolves were their only worry as they approached the city.

There was no need to search every block of Othium as they had in Lithus to find Marin. Before they even reached the city's edge, they saw a thick circle of black birds circling Princess Peridot's position. They flew overhead like an ominous thundercloud, guiding Emer and her friends to the sleeping princess.

"It's nearly sunset," Caden said, halting their group a few blocks away from the epicenter of animals. "Leo, do you know anything about wolf hunting?"

Leo gave Caden a sarcastic look. "Do you even need to ask? Wolves are usually nocturnal, but mostly active during dusk and dawn. Blackbirds—like crows and ravens—are diurnal, meaning that between the two of them, they have the whole guard shift. That

252

leaves the question; which type of animal are you more willing to fight?"

"Neither," Pearl whimpered. Mica shuddered to agree.

Leo grunted. "Birds might poke and scratch, but they're less likely to tear off your arms. Personally, I'd rather wait until the wolves are sleeping and face the birds."

Marin folded her arms. "Exactly how do you plan to 'face the birds?' Do you mean to kill innocent animals who protected our friends all these years? What if the wolves wake from the birds attacking us?"

"We fight," Leo said with a shrug. "I'm not waiting for a miracle, and I won't let Dot die."

"Then we camp here for the night." Caden dismounted and motioned to a nearby abandoned house that wasn't leaning or missing half of its roof. Unlike Somnus with its stone castles and thatched roofs, Ormio made their own stones as pale bricks, and their rooftops used planks instead of thatch work. The deciduous trees clustered closer to the abandoned buildings, leaving Emer unsure where the forest ended and the city proper began.

While gathering firewood, Emer asked Caden, "How do you propose we fight our way through an army of birds and wolves?"

He grunted. "We've been fairly lucky on timing with you and your sisters. The thorns gave way for me to pass through, the whirlpool stopped before it drowned you, and Pearl shone a light for Mica to lead us through the Midnight Forest. Maybe we'll get lucky again with these wolves."

"Except we were too late for Ruby," Emer said, spotting Leo already at the campsite, striking his whetstone toward some kindling. "I have a hard time imagining that many wild animals becoming docile as we encroach on their territory."

"Or they suddenly decide to abandon their territory as they did with Ruby. Who knows?" Caden shrugged. "We should have an advantage this time. Unlike unnatural thorns, water, and darkness, animals need to sleep and eat. We can try sneaking, but wolves will sense us by our smell or sound. It might be best to arrange a distraction to deviate a portion of the pack, then charge in with torches."

Leo grunted and shifted his eyes northward. "Wolves might be the least of our worries. This city is closer to Noz Isle. The mist is thickening again, and our horses are acting skittish like the first time the mære appeared. Also, my brother's still tracking us."

Emer half expected Caden to jokingly count off their various options for death, but he simply sank into the worries. Death was an all-too-real possibility after losing Ruby.

They set up camp and built a fire for the night. Yes, it made them more visible to Leo's sharp-shooting brother, but the fire would ward away the wolves. Maybe the mære too? Mica's stories made them seem invincible without weaknesses. Caden asked Emer to grow a hedge of thorns between them and the wolves as Ranae posted flaming staffs around their camp. Caden then encouraged Emer and her sisters to retire early to the coach, but they stood their ground for dinner outside.

Leo distributed a meatless dinner and frowned at their frightened group. Pointing at Pearl, he commanded, "Sing."

"Pardon?"

"Sing. Wolves howl to claim their territory or locate other wolves. Don't howl, but the more noise we make, the more likely they'll leave us alone."

"Oh, if you say so." Pearl began a sleepy lullaby, but Leo cut her off after the first stanza.

"Sing something jovial that others can join, dance, or laugh along. Make noise!"

Pearl switched to a sailing song, stomping her feet twice before two claps and two rest beats.

"With the wind in our sails and the sun on our side—"

Marin and Ranae grinned, recognizing the chant and joined, "We will see the whole world, no matter how wide."

They stopped to let Pearl begin the chanted list of places they each visited, "Like Somnus."

"And Lithus," Marin added.

Emer took a turn to add, "And Denebrae." She quickly explained the rules of the chant to Caden while Ranae took a turn. The chant would end if someone repeated a place, or the rhythm was broken.

Seeing his turn, Caden added the capital of Uldra, "And Veenigz."

Mica fumbled at his turn. "And Denebrae?"

"Oh!" Everyone else moaned at the broken chain before Marin and Ranae closed the song with its standard ending, "And many many more so long as we can reach their shores."

They tried again, going fully around their circle twice before Leo lost the rhythm. Their forced enthusiasm grew on them until it became genuine. Eventually completing a chain of five rounds, they switched to another song. The former sleepers all sang while the princes clapped, stomped their feet, or drummed on their knees. They swapped parts as Leo bellowed a poetic hunting tale, then Caden stood to begin a new piece.

"Hey, Jude," he began.

"Wait, I know this one," Mica said. "How do I know this one?"

"It's from England," Caden said, "by The Beatles. Funny name for a group of musicians, but I loved their music in my dreams."

Marin pursed her lips in thought. "I only heard a sample of England's music, and it thoroughly confused me. Please, sing on."

Caden sang, and Leo didn't stop him despite its slow beat. By the time he repeated the "Naaah-nah-nah" part twice, everyone was singing along, even Mica with his crooked pitch.

Eventually, their voices grew as tired as their bodies. The women were sent to sleep in the coach while the men hunkered around the camp.

Emer dreamed of waking Dot only to be eaten by wolves and poked at by birds. They tap-tap-tapped on her until she woke with a jolt. Her dreams followed her to reality as the tap-tap-tap continued against the coach door.

"Princesses?" Caden called after finishing his knocking. "Sorry to disturb your beauty sleep, but you're all lovely enough. We need to leave quickly to approach the wolves by midday."

Emer and her sisters battled between reluctance to wake and eagerness to find Dot. Dressed and half groomed, they joined the men for a cold breakfast.

Pearl raised a hand, as if asking for permission to speak. "I fear that I am less effective in battle, though I may assist Dot when she wakes. Returning to this altered reality is jarring, and a familiar face may be helpful."

"True," Marin said, "and untrue. Pearl, you can flash light at the animals to temporarily blind them or make them run and hide as in a thunderstorm. While Dot may appreciate a friendly face, you may command your light while safely situated in the coach."

"I agree," Caden said. "Emer, Marin, and Pearl, you'll be safest on the coach, outside the ring of animals, but close enough to use your magics. Leo should probably be the one to approach the inn. If he shared the dreams, then he should also be there when she wakes."

Leo's neck burned red. The more embarrassed he was, the more curious Emer became to learn what happened in his dreams with Ruby and Dot. As if she wasn't already anxious to wake Dot, Emer was eager to hear her perspective.

"Marin," Emer said, "could you create rain to enhance the storm illusion? Also, if you stay with Pearl and the coach, perhaps you can create a wall of ice to protect you and the horses."

"I—" she hesitated, "perhaps I can."

"You made a wall of ice when that ogre attacked you. I believe you can do it." Emer offered her older sister an encouraging smile.

Ranae stood to grab seconds, and added, "I can help Prince Leo reach the inn. Marin and Pearl can create the illusions of a thunderstorm, but will it be enough?"

"What if," Mica suggested, "we add a distraction to draw them away then trap them from quickly returning?"

Caden squirmed a little. "It needs to be someone who can set traps and climb trees very quickly."

"Why?" Pearl asked.

"Because," Emer said, "whoever causes the distraction will become the bait. Their job is to draw the wolves to them. If anything goes wrong, they will need to fight a pack on their own."

"Oh, Caden…" Mica hesitated. "If Leo and Ranae are fighting towards the inn, you're the best climber between the two of us, even with your injured arm."

"I know."

"I dislike this plan," Emer said, unable to stop herself. Drawing herself to her full height, she said, "If you must go, then so shall I."

"Please don't," he moaned. "You already almost died in Marin's whirlpool. Plus that swim in the lake—I can't handle you endangering yourself again."

"And if you never return to us," Emer argued, "how will we know if you were eaten or simply lost? I may have been raised in a different forest, but I can ask the plants to create the trap, help you up a tree, and direct us back to the group."

"She has a point," Mica said.

"Also," Emer added, "I am the fastest runner among the women here. Marin is your best swimmer, and Pearl is your most graceful presence, but when it comes to climbing trees," she dropped into a Cockney accent for dramatic effect to say, "you won't be left Jack Jones." She would never leave Caden alone in danger.

Pearl giggled while Marin's face went eschewed. Emer paid them no attention as she kept her determined eyes on Caden.

He relented with a heavy sigh. "I can't convince you to stay?"

"No. I want to help you, Caden. You, my sisters, and my friends. No matter the risk."

"Then let's trap the wolves like babblin' brooks." He smirked.

Emer grinned. Yes, they would trap them like crooks. "Let me change into something more appropriate for climbing."

Dashing to the coach, she overheard Marin whisper to Pearl, "Was that supposed to make sense?"

"I learned a couple of odd interpretations for words in my dreams, though nothing that confusing."

Inside the coach, Emer removed many of her underlayers to wear a simple tanned chemise, topped with a green kirtle. She hoped the colors would help her blend into the forest, though maybe it didn't matter since she remembered hearing somewhere that wolves were colorblind. More importantly, she and Caden needed to wash their scents.

Going back to Marin, she asked for her to create a stream for them. Her older sister raised an eyebrow.

"What makes you think I would disrupt the natural ecosystem?"

Emer groaned. "Then could you at least tell us where to find a nearby stream?"

Marin opened her mouth to debate her capabilities, but Ranae jumped in. "Probably. What was that trick you did to find Ruby? You connected with the trees?"

"I connected to one tree, and it linked me to all of the surrounding plants. Maybe if you find wet soil, you can do the same."

Marin looked doubtful, but Ranae urged her. "Give it a try."

With a deep breath, Marin flexed her hands, and shook them loose. "Alright, I shall try."

Pressing her palm to the ground, she closed her eyes and frowned in concentration.

Emer waited, and waited…and waited. "Is it working?"

"Hush," Marin said. After another few seconds, Marin opened her eyes and stood. Pointing to the east, she said, "There is a canal that empties into the lake that way. It is shallow from new dams, though should be sufficient."

"I knew you could do it." Ranae grinned.

Emer thanked her and ran off to Caden. "Marin said there is a canal that way. We can use it to wash our scents before causing the distraction."

"Brilliant," Caden said. "Shall we go then?"

"Hey," Mica called to them, "I hope you didn't forget about the last time you two went on an adventure together. Neither of you are allowed to die, remember?"

"Don't you know, Mica?" Caden teased. "I plan to live forever."

"Forever?" Emer laughed.

"So far so good." He winked. "Come on, let's go distract and trap a horde of wolves."

Chapter 20

EMER

Grabbing one end of the vine phone, Emer and Caden ran eastward through Othium. After dunking themselves in the neglected canal, they ran to the outskirts of the city, stretching the vine phone to its full length. They picked their layout, agreed on a plan, then Emer spoke to the plants. Within the hour, they had a covered pit trap and a hunter's nest in a sturdy tree.

Caden's eyebrows went high. "If you were trying to impress me, you succeeded."

Emer grinned back. "See? You needed me."

"Really, you overdid yourself. This is more than we'll need, and I've never seen your plants move that quickly."

Indeed, Emer wondered if her connection with the plants had strengthened from her dives into their roots. "All the better if we want to reach Dot today. Up you go," she said, gesturing to their hunter's nest.

Caden tested each branch before using it to brace himself, favoring his left arm, then watched to make sure Emer made each step safely. As soon as they left the ground, Emer asked the tree to grow taller with tougher bark to keep the wolves from reaching them in the nest.

Secure in their nest of criss-crossing branches, Emer asked the mushrooms to release perfumes that smelled of fresh meat.

"Brilliant," Caden said. "Let's see if I can make the right sound to lure them."

Moaning around his hands, he made a rather pitiful sound to imitate an injured moose.

"Oh!" Marin's voice cried from the phone. "What poor animal is that supposed to be?"

Emer chuckled as Caden adjusted his hands to change the sound.

Leo's voice echoed through the vine next. "One reason wolves howl is to claim their territory. Make them think there's competition."

Caden shrugged then moaned a long howl at the direction they came.

"Not bad," Emer teased. "May I try?"

"How often does a princess get to howl?"

"Not often enough."

She howled, crying her voice into the air, letting it take all her frustrations and fears. Seeing Caden's raised smile and eyebrows, she struggled not to end her howl with a laugh.

One wolf, then a second joined.

"Good," Leo said. "Now, act like that impetuous uncle who cuts across every conversation."

Caden howled back, interrupting their calls with aggression.

Three howls became an indistinguishable amount as they howled over one another.

Marin took over the phone duty to report, "You have their attention. Several wolves rose from their nap and ran in your direction. Be careful."

"Several?" Emer echoed. "Is it enough?"

"It better be," Caden said, "I don't have any better ideas."

"Now what do we do?"

"We wait."

"And what do we do while we wait?"

He raised a flirtatious corner of his eyebrow and mouth. "I can think of a couple things."

"We can still hear you," Marin scolded.

Emer smirked and nudged Caden's arm with a light tease. "We need to stay alert."

As they waited, clouds gathered around the circling blackbirds. Light flashed soundlessly to signal the start of their approach to the inn. The lured wolves arrived soon after.

They surrounded the pungent mushrooms, and Emer counted them. "Only eleven?"

"That's a large pack to hunt a wounded animal or fight off trespassers."

"Should we wait for more to arrive?" she asked. "Is this enough to let Leo and Ranae break into the inn?"

Marin spoke through the phone, "They started to push into the pack. Pearl and I are safe atop the carriage and Mica is serving as a minor distraction on the fringes. Their progress…barely meets the definition of progress."

Caden signaled for Emer to begin the next phase of their plan.

"Vines below the wolves," Emer said, "pull away!"

The crisscrossing vines beneath the wolves' feet slipped back to reveal the pit beneath them. The wolves yelped as they fell. It wasn't enough to fatally injure them, but would confine them for a few hours before they dug their way out. Marin had approved of their trap.

"Now, we return to help the others?"

Caden nodded. "Back to the inn like the devil's hounds are on our tails."

They carefully descended the tree and stepped around the wolf pit. The wolves had already scratched their way into one side of the pit in their attempts to escape.

Emer wrapped the phone vine around her arm as it directed their path back to the inn.

The trapped wolves began barking while the wolves ahead howled. It seemed that striking during their naptime had only been somewhat effective.

"Come on!" Caden urged, pulling her faster.

Emer ran, struggling to pick up and carry the phone vine in her haste. She wanted to be there to help the others. She ran until an uneasy feeling slithered up her spine. A growl sounded to her right through the trees. That couldn't be good.

"Caden?" She slowed to search for the wolf in the woods. Where was it? Was it alone or with a pack?

"It seems the trapped pack called for help."

"And we ran right into them?"

Caden grunted to affirm. "On a positive note, it means we did better than we thought at drawing more wolves away from the inn."

"Glad to be of help," she panted, half out of breath and half for terror. She palmed a tree to ask for the locations of the wolves. There were six surrounding them from every side. She pointed their positions to Caden. "What do we do? We cannot run without starting a chase."

He growled. "I suddenly wish you'd stayed at the coach again. Do we have any choices other than to fight or die trying?"

"Climb a tree and wait for Dot's curse to release them?"

"With my arm? You'd probably make it. Besides, we don't know what will happen to the animals when Dot wakes."

Emer grimaced. Leaving him below wasn't an option, and she had no idea how the wolves would react to Dot's awakening. They could continue to hunt her and Caden as wild animals.

Caden waved his arms wide and shouted, "We can try to intimidate them with loud noises like last night."

Yes, and there was another option…

While Caden shouted to make himself seem bigger, Emer called, "Vines, wrap around the legs of waiting wolves. Hold them still."

"Good idea," Caden said, unsheathing his sword. "Did that give us any openings?"

"This way!" She stepped to her right. She wanted to run through the opening while it was still there, but she kept her eyes on the visible wolves. Together, they continued to make large noises and motions while stepping carefully to the side. But they couldn't watch all of the wolves at once.

A wolf leapt at her, but Caden jumped over to meet its challenge with a swipe of his sword. Releasing his attention, two more wolves jumped in from behind. He turned back, catching a bite above his ankle while stabbing a wolf in the shoulder. He bellowed his agony while swinging his sword to ward off the next attack. Emer's vines had caught two wolves, and the wounded one retreated, but three more continued to growl and circle them. Emer grabbed a stick from the ground and waved it back and forth at the wolves, wishing she had something better.

A wolf cry rose from the direction of the inn, and the remaining three wolves halted their attacks. With raised ears and noses pointed toward the inn, they ran away.

"Beshrews," Caden cursed. "The others need our help."

"Can you still run?" Emer nodded toward his bleeding leg.

He grimaced as he limped forward. Emer slipped under his arm, and together, they hobbled back to their friends.

They entered the city borders again and ran around the abandoned buildings to reach the inn. They stepped into a storming warzone. Thunderclouds poured from above, scattering the birds to their nests. Flashes of light blinded them like lightning without thunder. The wolves ran around, disoriented, but still determined to keep Leo and Ranae away from the inn entrance.

Caden began to limp forward, but Emer grabbed his hand to hold him back. "What are you doing?"

"Going to help," Caden said, then smirked. "Wait, are you being overprotective of me now?"

"Irritating, right?"

He laughed. "I'm a prince. It's my job to protect others. Besides, you can command the plants from afar, but I have to fight up close and personal."

She hated the truth of his words. His sword wasn't a long-range weapon.

"What about your wounds?"

"It's just a—"

"Flesh wound," she finished with him, keeping her hand around his. "Stop lying about your injuries or you might make them worse!"

"True, the phrase was originally spoken by a man with both of his arms cut off, but if you can't sit back and watch others struggle, what makes you think I can? Even Mica's fighting on the fringes to distract the wolves. Also," he leaned in close, locking her gaze, "I'm a historian. You know I need to be on the front row of history in the making when we find Princess Peridot."

She groaned. "You can be such a dolt sometimes. Fine." She released him. "But let me clear a way first."

He nodded and stepped back as Emer talked to the plants, asking vines to trail between them and the inn entrance.

"Good," she encouraged the plants. "Now, grow thorns large enough to become spikes. Block the wolves from entering your path that we may pass through unharmed."

Thorns grew up and outward, defining the path to the door. Wolves yelped and leapt away. Leo noticed the opportunity and jumped into the trench sanctuary. His advance to the door increased.

Equine screams of drowning horses cried in the distance. Shadows rose from the edge of the lake. The mære were coming.

"Emer," Caden said, "I don't know if we have the time for this."

Leo shot an arrow at the distant mære. It slipped right through it with barely a break of smoke. Leo swore and tried again with the same results.

He gave up and returned his focus to the inn. Emer agreed. If they couldn't fight the oncoming mære, they had to find Dot, grab her, then leave before the mære reached them.

"Go, Caden!" she cheered him with an encouraging push toward the thorny trench.

Caden graced her with a quick kiss, then ran between the posts of thorns. The wolves snarled and swiped their claws at him as he passed, but mostly remained outside the path.

Emer ran to join Pearl and Marin as they stood on top of the carriage, enclosed by ice. Marin melted a section of the ice to let Emer through, then quickly rebuilt it. From the top of the carriage, Emer spotted Caden and Leo as they reached the inn door. Before she could cheer for joy, Marin called, "Ranae! Mica! Fall back!"

Both men looked relieved to retreat. They were both tired from fighting the wolves, not even noticing the black shadows of mære coming fast from the lake.

"Please," Emer prayed. "Wake up, Dot." She didn't want to stick around for another encounter with the mære, and she couldn't handle the thought of losing another friend.

Chapter 21

DOT

When Mom started packing our things with the threat of leaving, I realized how comfortable we'd become in Texas (notwithstanding the lump underneath me). We'd really settled into the room, using the drawers and scattering our belongings into the bathroom. Mom told me not to feel guilty about making ourselves at home because our presence had turned the bachelor house into a home with a feminine touch. I did what I could to help pack on the bed, though my movements were painful and lethargic. Miserable as I was, I didn't want to leave without seeing Leo one more time (if only to say goodbye). I even wanted to say goodbye to Ruby. I still felt bitter toward her, but I hoped for reconciliation (somehow).

To my surprise, Mom was also a reluctant packer. It wasn't until Dad poked his head into the room and Mom's face brightened that I realized why. She would miss him. I was deaf, but I wasn't blind to their flirtatious expressions.

Mom and Dad spoke for a few measures before she translated for me. He was willing to make an exception to allow Leo to see me.

We agreed to stay for at least one meeting, but I hesitated to see him. At first, it was because I was still upset. Even if he hadn't consented to the kiss, he'd let Ruby touch his face. What had he expected? Second, I hesitated because I didn't know what to say to him. Even if I forgave and forgot the stolen kiss, where did our relationship stand?

I hardly knew him outside of my dream's memories and our previous conversations through the window. I knew he was a good man, and knowing his good nature made me hope for more.

I remembered his signs after the kiss, "I love *you*, Dot." But did I love him? Sure, the sight of him made my heart flutter, and (after telling Mom about what happened with Ruby), she helped me realize that I could (eventually) live with Leo ending up with Ruby. The mere thought of it hurt like slanders, but...I wanted him to be happy after I woke up. Reluctantly, Mom admitted that my desire for his happiness over my own meant that I truly did love him.

It was almost another week before I opened the curtains fully to spot the men having lunch. Leo straightened at my movement and asked to switch seats with the worker in the corner with the best view to me.

"Dot!" he signed eagerly. Slanders, he was magnificently built. I suddenly pitied Ruby that she couldn't see the way his muscles moved as he smoothly signed, "How are you?"

I gave him a downward stare. "How do you think?"

He grimaced. "Sorry."

I wasn't in the mood to unload my complaints of bruises from the bed, occasional agony from my broken foot, or burning heartache from his face. I released a heavy breath and asked, "How are you?"

"Depressed," he said. "I want to see you."

"You see me now."

He rolled his eyes. "I want to talk face to face, in the same room. My boss says I'm allowed. Only me. Because of you. Please?"

I chewed on my cheek. "Maybe tomorrow."

His face lit with such hope and joy that it hurt like staring at the sun.

He bounced his fingers at me for my attention again, and asked, "What was your homeland called again?"

"O-R-M-I-O," I fingerspelled.

"Not U-L-D-R-A?"

I gaped. "No. U-L-D-R-A's North, above R-E-Z-H-I-N-A Valley. How do you know that name?"

"Really?" He sat back a little dazed. "Shino had a dream last night about a place named U-L-D-R-A. He said he saw a flag." He used classifying signs to visually draw the flag in the air with green on top, a white bottom, and a gold line across the middle.

"Yes, yes! That's U-L-D-R-A!" I signed quickly with enthusiasm. Strange how a foreign kingdom could remind me so much of home. It was close enough. With Ruby's silence, only the birds knew how much I missed my real family. Would Leo understand? I asked, "Did Shino say more about his dream of U-L-D-R-A?"

"He told me about it," Leo signed, frowning. "He looked…haunted."

"Why?"

"He died."

I blinked, and hesitated to ask, "How?"

"His English is so-so, but he said something about fighting green giants in a 'big house for kings.' Maybe a castle? He said he died in honor, protecting his men and helping his friends, including me." Leo smirked. "He said I was a prince or something. Crazy, right?"

What could that mean? Had Shino somehow gone to Uldra as Ruby and I had come to America? And what was Leo doing there? Could he be real in Uldra?

Or was it no more than a dream? Shino had died in his dream, but he seemed fine here. Did that mean Ruby and I could be dead in Ormio?

Slanders, I hoped not.

Not knowing what to say, I signed, "There are worse ways to go." Like lying in bed, wasting away until these bruises made it hurt to move. I never knew that lying around could be so painful.

We continued to sign through the window (talking about anything except our feelings) until he returned to work. I spent the rest of the day worrying about my appearance. I asked my mom to carry me to the bathtub, and I washed myself with a flower-scented soap. Slanders, I was covered in hideous bruises. The past several days, I'd stayed in my sleeping gown, but for Leo's visit, I wore my favorite dress. It was the same peridot green as my eyes with little blue birds spotting its pattern. Not even reading could distract me from my frenzied thoughts as I waited for Leo's lunch visit.

He walked in and my nervous smile collapsed into a frown as my blind sister followed.

"Why's she here?" I signed.

"Her dad made an exception for me to visit you, but I can't be alone in a room with women on the property. It's for everyone's protection."

Yes, that made sense. It was also an excuse to never let me be alone with Leo.

"Fine," I signed and resituated toward Ruby, "then let's theorize how to wake up and leave this nightmare."

Leo translated between us as Ruby frowned. "Why?"

"Why?" I asked, incredulous. "Do you honestly never want to wake up?"

"No, this is my home," she said. "I'm needed here more than in Ormio. Dad needs me to take care of the house, and someone needs to make sure that Mom and Dad get together. Don't you want to stay here with Leo?"

Leo's eyebrow was habitually raised with wide-eyed confusion as he translated our conversation, but the last "yes or no" question raised both eyebrows with earnest curiosity.

I wasn't sure how to answer that even if he hadn't been in the room. Hands trembling, I signed, "I don't belong here. From the moment I arrived, I heard nothing but screams and felt nothing but pain. It doesn't matter what Peridot feels for Leo, he deserves someone who can live and enjoy life. Whether that's Dorothy, the woman he first fell in love with...or you, Ruby."

Leo translated to my sister, but instead of finishing with the option to be with Ruby, he tilted his head at me. "Peridot?"

I nodded. "That's my real name, but I liked the name Dot, like your Dorothy."

He stared at the ground thoughtfully. As much as I wanted to talk with him privately, there were words that Ruby needed first.

"Ruby," I signed, "I'm sorry."

I watched Leo mouth the words, and Ruby's face constricted with confusion.

"For what?" Leo translated for me, though his wide eyes suggested his own curiosity.

"I used you," I signed. "I wanted you to want what I had. If I went for something and you didn't care, I wanted it less. When you wanted something that I had, I valued it more. And I may have been a little vindictive in holding onto things, knowing you wanted them."

Ruby folded her arms and smirked in a way that was both victorious and annoyed. "I knew it."

"In a way," Leo spoke and signed, "it's a compliment. You wanted Ruby's validation and approval. You valued her opinion."

I smiled at his attempt to make it seem less awful. "Still," I signed, "that doesn't make it right. That's why I'm sorry, Ruby."

I watched her chest rise and fall with a deep breath. She unfolded her arms to place her hands on her hips. "Fine. It won't matter if you go back to Washington or Ormio, anyway. You can have Leo and anything you want wherever you go as long as I get anything I want in Texas."

"I can agree to that." I grinned, but had to ask, "What about Mom and Dad?"

"Obviously Dad can't sell the farm, but Mom can do her woodworking anywhere, so she'll stay here."

I frowned. "Why do you get Mom?"

"I knew you'd ask that. It's only fair, because you'll leave her anyway when you marry Leo or go back to Ormio." Leo pinched back an uneasy smile and added, "Do I have a say in this?"

Despite his tease, I saw the subtle doubt in his question. The only part that involved him was marrying me. Did he want to break our engagement?

Hesitating with small signs, I asked Leo, "Can we talk alone?"

His expression doubted the possibility, but he asked Ruby.

Ruby answered him with a downward stare. Folding her arms, she spoke and Leo translated, "No. House rules. We already made an exception for you two. You're welcome, by the way. Besides, I can't see your secret hand signs, anyway. You two can have a perfectly secretive mushy gushy conversation even with me in the room." After translating, Leo added, "She's not wrong."

"I don't need anything mushy gushy," I signed directly to Leo. "Just…truth. After all that happened these last few weeks, with me stuck in bed while you work day after day…I've had a lot of time to ponder. I know you mattered a lot to Dorothy, and with her memories in my head, you mean a lot to me too. But I need to wake up and return to Ormio. I don't know if Dorothy will still be here when I leave."

He frowned as if my words hurt him. "Dot, I gave you that ring with a promise; that in two years, when you're graduated and I've earned enough for the both of us, I want to marry you. I don't know everything that's going on between you and Ruby and your out-of-this-world life…but we have two years to work it out. Together. As long as Dorothy's still a part of who you are, I want to be a part of your life. I love you."

It became difficult to watch his signs between my blurring eyes. I smiled, relieved by his kindness, understanding, and love. The future had too many options to know what would happen, but I knew one thing as I looked into his determined light brown eyes; Leo would be fine.

"You're a good man," I signed. "I'd be lucky to have you."

I reached for his cheek, caressing his fuzzy beard, and drew him to me. As if we'd done it a dozen times before (because Dorothy had), Leo met me halfway, pressing his lips to mine.

With my eyes closed and my ears ringing, there was suddenly nothing around us. Just Leo and me, alone in a world of our own creation. We could have been anywhere: a guest bedroom in Texas, our favorite park in Washington, or even an Ormio inn with a ridiculous amount of mattresses.

When his lips left mine and I opened my eyes, that was where I was.

Chapter 22

DOT

From the top of a dozen mattresses, Dot opened her eyes to find a man's face in her periphery.

With heavy arms, Dot signed his name. "Leo."

He had the same brown eyes, stiff nose, and thin smile. His long brown hair was a little loose from a low ponytail, and his beard was a week longer and more scruffy than in her dream. He leaned back to sign, "Dot?"

"What kind of code is that?"

Dot jumped at the audio. A voice. Another man stood at the doorway. He had black hair with a trimmed beard around his rectangular face and wore the green and white colors of Uldra. More importantly—

She heard him speak! The ringing screams were gone!

"It's sign language," a deep voice said beside her.

Dot turned back to Leo. She'd never heard him speak before, but the vibrations from his deep timbre were the same.

"Leo?" she rasped out loud.

"Dot?" He blinked, surprised. "You can talk?"

"And hear," she said, struggling to clear her throat. Why did it feel so dry? Leo offered her a waterskin. She closed her eyes while she drank, trying to ignore the man staring at her like a menagerie act, soaking in the sounds of her own breathing and some chaos outside. She couldn't keep her eyes closed for long. She opened them to make sure Leo was still there. He wasn't just a dream.

Holding the empty waterskin in her lap, Dot asked, "What happened? How are you in Ormio?"

"It's a long story," Leo said, reaching for her to take his hand. "First, let's get you down from here. Caden, what are the birds and wolves doing?"

"Birds?" she asked as she pushed herself to sit up. She immediately collapsed, sore like she'd been beaten by a Huiess fighter.

"They—they're standing by, like they're waiting for orders. The mære are slaughtering them! They'll reach us if we don't hurry!"

Dot had no idea what "mære" were, but the man's words made sense of the noise outside. Birds and dogs squawked and cried in pain. Hearing the slaughter struck her heart with terror.

"No!" she cried, her voice hoarse. "They should fight back! Don't let them kill them! Fight back or fly away if they cannot!"

The man named Caden at the door took a step back with wide eyes as he stared at the scene outside. He turned his surprised eyes to Dot and smiled. "Brilliant! She can influence animals! The birds and wolves are following her commands!"

Leo's jaw dropped. "The animals can hurt the mære? And you have a magical influence over animals? I don't remember that happening in the dream."

"I—what? I have no magic," Dot said.

"The animals…" The man at the door paused as he stared outside. "So, some of them can fight the mære." He seemed too preoccupied with studying the battle to explain further, letting Leo's attention turn back to Dot and her weak attempts to scoot out of bed. She'd managed to slide away from the perturbing lump, but the pain remained like a phantom bruise on her left shoulder blade.

"Here, let me help you," Leo said, scooping her into his arms. He was just as she had dreamed: strong, bold, and loving.

With her face close to his, their gazes locked for a long second.

Her face burned brightly. He shifted her to the edge of the mattresses, then carefully stepped down the step-stool, bracing both their bodies against the bars.

Reaching the ground, Leo said, "Sorry to kiss and run, but the mære are coming."

"Mære?" she asked, testing her feet against the wood flooring. No pebble. No bruises. No broken foot. No screams. But also no strength. She started to collapse, but Leo held her upright in his arms.

"So," Caden said, "if she can influence birds and wolves, it's possible she can influence all animals. Does that include mære?"

"Whoever said I could influence animals?" she asked.

"No one," Leo chuckled. "You just did it. Here, try commanding those black beasts to stand down."

He escorted her to the door, opening her view to a different kind of nightmare. Her time in Texas had been miserable, true, but it had also been beautiful to watch from her window. This place was the exact opposite. Her beloved city of Othium had been neglected, crumbled, and overrun with plants and warring animals. She stared in horror as birds and large dogs attacked shadow monsters. The animals hardly seemed to touch them as the monsters attacked back with deadly slashes.

"No!" Dot cried. "Stop!"

The birds and dogs obeyed, but the monsters continued. One slash was enough to change her command. "No! Attack! Defend yourselves!"

The animals returned to their fight.

"Wow," a female voice said nearby. Emer? How was she awake? And Marin—and Pearl! The Somnus Princesses smiled at her.

Dot cried for joy and stumbled toward them. The other princesses caught her in an embrace.

Caden frowned at them. "I thought you were supposed to stay safe on the coach."

Pearl answered with a beaming smile at Dot. "As soon as the wolves and birds changed their attacks, we knew it was time to greet our friend."

Emer said, "I expected your magic to involve animals since they surrounded you, but to see magic in action is always a wonder."

"I have no idea what's happening, but I'm so glad to see you!" Dot cried.

"Yes, yes," Marin said with a light laugh, "it is good to see you too. However, first things first—Shield us!"

Water surged from the ground and instantly solidified into ice. Emer called upon vines that crawled across the inn to weave around the monster's ankles. Pearl commanded soundless lightning to flash across the monsters' eyes, though only a few of the animals managed to halt the monsters.

Dot gaped. "How long was I asleep?"

"Longer than you think," Emer said. "But what matters is that you are awake now. Can you help us find Garnet?"

"Garnet?" Dot repeated, half dazed. "We planned to warn my parents in Veriae."

The sisters shared an uncomfortable and worried look.

"What?" Dot asked.

Emer shuffled. "Veriae was destroyed by the monsters that attack us now."

Dot's heart dropped to her feet. Her home? All those people? The bakery on Speare Lane? The aviary of domesticated birds? What about the castle? The fortress had held strong against countless attacks from Huiess. It couldn't have fallen…could it?

Staring at the black monsters, she couldn't doubt their strength and strange defensive abilities. Her fury built within her until it exploded with a screaming command, "Attack! Chase them out of this city!"

The large dogs and black birds attacked with vigor. Emer, Marin, and Pearl watched in frightened awe as sounds of chaos grew around them. Rats scurried from the abandoned buildings. Badgers and other scavengers bound into the fray as moose and elk charged from the forest with horns lowered. The fighting men yelped and retreated to the inn to join the stares.

Not all the animal attacks were effective, but the horde swarmed the monsters. The black nightmares attacked ferociously until something seemed to call them away. Like a switch, they all turned and retreated to the lake.

A young man next to Pearl was the first to shout for victory. Leo, Caden, and Admiral Ranae joined as the Somnus sisters cried for joy, embracing Dot once again. The animals continued to chase the monsters until Dot called them off. She was far from satisfied, but there was no need to injure more animals in the fight. Turning back to her friends, she had to verify, "Is it true? Veriae was destroyed?"

A few of them turned to Caden. (Apparently, he was the one with answers.) He pressed his mouth into a grim line and nodded. "Yes, but if that's where Garnet went, then that's where we'll go. We need to wake her and your sisters if we're going to take this land back. We won't let Queen Tanzi take anyone else."

"Anyone else?" Dot asked. Looking around, she realized someone was missing. If all the Somnus sisters were awake— "Where's Ruby?"

Chapter 23

RUBY

The silent conversation between Dot and Leo became too silent. Their hands no longer slapped or slid against each other. I might have worried about them kissing, but the bed didn't even creak with shifting weight. They no longer made breathy expressions with half-spoken words. They no longer breathed.

"Dot?" I asked the room. Dumb question. She couldn't hear me to answer. "Leo?"

No response.

I stepped forward and swung my stick ahead of me until I hit the legs of the bedframe. I swept it all the way beneath the bed.

"Leo?" I asked. "Where did you go?"

Silence.

Careful to feel my stick upward against the bed frame, I found the top and slid it across. I expected to hit Leo's back or side, but found only wrinkled blankets.

Either Dot and Leo were lying impossibly flat, or they'd left the bed. How? Dot had been immobile. If Leo had picked her up and walked anywhere, I would have heard.

"Rayban!" I called. Within the second, the jingle of his collar joined my side. "Find Leo."

Rayban whined and remained by my side. Slanders, what did he mean by that?

"Dad!" I called. "Rayban, find Dad!"

His collar jingled as his paws scampered out of the room and through the flip-flap of the back doggy-door.

I remained in the room, sweeping my stick across the floor, over the beds, tapping against the closed window…Nothing.

Mom—er—Candi arrived first. Dad wasn't far behind. They asked me where Dot was.

"I don't know. She was signing with Leo, then they just disappeared." I gave them the details of my search, and they began a search through the house. The workday was canceled as Dad recruited the employees to help search the grounds. All the vehicles were accounted for. Candi called the cops, and I gave my "witness" account three more times throughout the day.

I was fairly certain I knew the truth; she woke up. She returned to Ormio. I wasn't sure how she took

Leo with her and couldn't explain any of it to the cops, so I told them only the facts.

By nightfall, Leo and Dot were nowhere to be found, and Candi cried into Dad's arms. She cried until she fell asleep on the couch. She probably didn't want to return to the guest bedroom that she'd shared with Dot.

I cried in my own room. Despite our fights, I missed my twin and hoped she'd be well without me. Would she tell the others that I'd miss them? I hoped they'd understand.

The next day went by with cops and neighbors checking on us, offering hopeful reports despite their lack of results. I tried to encourage Candi with my hope that Dot was awake and happy in Ormio. The words felt true in my bones and eased my own pain, but did little to soothe Mom.

After the third day, Candi packed for Washington. "If she went anywhere on her own, it would have been back to Washington. It's home."

I mentally disagreed. Dot's home was Ormio. She loved the hustle and bustle of Veriae's fortress, of Othium's docks, and of Noz Isle's midnight masquerades. She had preferred the duties of a princess over the quiet country life.

My heart ached to miss her and our friends, but my home was with the quiet cotton fields, my hard working dad, and my most loyal doggy friend. Home was where the dog-hair stuck to everything…except the dog.

"I understand," Dad said, carrying Mom's luggage to her car. "Keep me updated if you find anything. I'm worried about your daughter, but I'll also want to reprimand Leo for going AWOL."

"Thanks, Eric. I'll keep in touch."

I caught a hint of a smile in her voice before she shut her car door and drove away.

Days passed. Mom and Dad called each other frequently for updates. Their calls stretched longer every night as they continued their conversations to happier topics. I smiled at that.

A week after Dot and Leo's disappearance, Dad hired a new employee to help with the crops. He spoke loudly like Leo, but unlike Leo, he spoke a lot.

Despite Dot and Leo's disappearance, life continued as usual. The harvest waited for no one. I worked on my crochet project on the back porch while Shino practiced reading an English book aloud. Being under eighteen meant he was a part-time worker, and apparently he'd spent most of his days in his cottage, reading and practicing English. Ever since Leo's replacement, however, he took to reading on the main house back porch. At first, it was to find a quiet place for practicing English. Then, it was to listen to me play my trumpet. When I discovered his regular presence, I joined him in the afternoons to crochet and to listen to (sometimes correcting) his reading.

He was about to pick up John Steinbeck's "The Pearl" after lunch, when the other workers chuckled and whispered from beyond the porch. I got the sense that they were talking about me, but I ignored them. I didn't care what anyone thought of me. Except dogs. I wanted all dogs to love me.

"Jose," the new loud worker said, "you should ask her out. You're a match made in heaven because she can't see how ugly you are."

"Shut up. If ugliness is the biggest factor, then that would make you the perfect match, you—"

Bam!

I jumped as something solid smacked into the paneled wall by my left ear. Rayban's collar jingled as he moved with surprise.

"What was that?" I shrieked.

The despicable men had initially gone silent from the slam, but then burst into laughter—probably from my pathetic shriek.

"Ah," Shino said, closer to me than I'd expected. "*Kabedon.* I guess it works better on TV."

"Works? To do what? Was there a bug on the wall behind me or something?"

"Aaah," Shino drew out his words into a slurred, "Yes."

What an obvious lie. Then there was no bug. Why had he slammed the wall so close to my face then? Seeing no real cause for alarm, Rayban rested his chin on my leg again, helping me to calm down.

I mentally repeated the unknown word Shino used until I had the chance to ask my virtual assistant about it.

"One usage," it said, "as it often appears in manga or anime, is when a male character corners a love interest against a wall and hits the wall to bar them in, creating a 'don' sound."

Love interest? My face warmed.

I could see the situation all too clearly in my head. There we'd been, sitting on the porch bench against the house as the other workers teased me. Shino slammed the wall with his arm and fist to get their attention and probably gave them a good glare. Then, with his arm barred around me, his action became a proclamation of protection and possession.

Except there was one part of the scene that was still blurry in my mind. I didn't know exactly what Shino looked like.

It took me all night and the next morning to plan my wording and gather courage before approaching the subject after lunch.

"I looked up *Kabedon*," I told him after we sat on the bench.

He said nothing. He also didn't ignore me and start reading, so I continued, "Shino, do you like me?"

"Ah…" He shuffled, but said no more.

Taking a deep breath and hoping I spoke correctly, I said a phrase in Japanese, "Love and a cough cannot be hidden."

I really wished to see how wide his eyes became as he spouted a stream of quick sentences I didn't understand.

"Whoa! Slow down. I only started last week." Other than the one phrase, I could barely ask for water and say "Mr. Nakayama is a funny teacher." I was about to tell him as much as I raised my hands to slow his words, but my raised hand slipped against his arm.

He was so close.

"Um, Shino?" I swallowed and forced myself to speak. "May I feel the contours of your face? I promise not to get carried away." Again.

"Yes," he said quietly. His trembling hand cupped my wrist and slowly guided me to his face. While Leo had tolerated my touch, Shino welcomed me. Nervous and shy, yet welcoming.

I kept one hand at his bony jaw while my other slid down to his shoulder. He wasn't nearly as large as Leo, though still a little taller than I was. Shino was

296

thinner than Leo, but just as muscled, proven by his solid and wide shoulders. Back up to his face, I was surprised to find round cheeks, set higher than Leo's. Unlike Leo, Shino was clean shaven, and his ears were rounder. The tips of his straight thick hair were trimmed close to the skin above his neck, though a finger-width longer on his top. He had no signs of premature balding.

He was handsome. In an adorable sense. While Leo had felt like a German Shepherd with his large build and edge of intriguing danger, Shino was more like a Beagle; friendly and emotionally sensitive.

"Soft hands," he said.

"Not awkward?" I asked. I'd made it awkward with Leo.

"No," he said.

Without saying more, I wasn't sure how he actually felt about the situation. I pulled my hands away, but he caught one with his own. As if I'd shocked him, he let go and shuffled back, mumbling, "Sorry."

"Sorry?" I asked. The moment had been nice until he shied back like he didn't deserve to speak his mind. I struggled to keep back my irritation as I asked, "Sorry, for what? For being nice to me? For acting for yourself?"

"No, that is not what I mean—"

"And this is exactly what *I* mean! Why won't you just say what you mean? You almost did that day when you found me crying. And I'm sorry I shut you down, but things were different then. I was heart-broken and jealous, but I've accepted it. I moved on. Why haven't you tried again?"

"Because I do not know," he murmured. "I do not know what I feel—I do not know how to describe it."

"Use words!"

He spewed a string of words in his native tongue.

"Yes! I don't care if I don't understand you, I need to hear you. Say what you feel and slanders to being 'proper!'"

"It hurts!"

His burst lingered in the air as I was unsure how to respond. I hurt him? "How?"

He groaned with frustration. "Always. I ache when we are away, and I am afraid when we are together."

"Afraid?"

"Yes."

"How?" I asked again.

He shuffled uneasily. "I am afraid I will do something that creates dislike."

"What could you possibly do to make me dislike you?"

He went so still and silent that I almost thought he'd gone. Then, he said, "Hold…you."

I hadn't realized it until that moment, but that was the first time I'd ever heard him say "you." As if the simple pronoun was too personal—too intimate—for casual use. Coming from Shino, the word was like a love confession more than his stated desire to hold me.

I'd expected my heart to become tense from this realization. Instead, it felt freed.

"You already did that," I said. "I'm still here."

"Then," he began, "it did not create dislike?"

"It meant the world to me. I wanted to make sure it meant something to you too."

"It means everything. It makes the hurting stop."

"I do not want to hurt you," I said, scooting closer to his voice. "You also make my pain go away."

Dot chose to leave and somehow took Leo with her, but I chose to stay there…with my dad…with Shino. I really liked Shino. Not in the way I thought I loved Leo, but more…well, I had to agree with Shino that it was hard to describe.

While I'd been initially attracted to both men, I'd focused on Leo because he was taken by Dot. But I chose Shino because he was genuine. There was no jealousy concerning him, only trust.

Shino tenderly slid his hand around mine. His touch was achingly slow as my heart pounded as fast as Rayban's. I thought about grabbing his hand sooner, then realized his slowness wasn't out of fear or timidness, but respect.

I wasn't a princess in Texas, but Shino still treated me like one. Perhaps, there was a lesson in there for me to respect myself and others the same way.

Yes, I could happily spend the rest of my life in this place.

Epilogue

TANZI

Queen Tanzanite stared into the black abyss, and it stared back through a mære's eyes. The one in front of her had its leg almost chomped off. Some wolf had served a lucky strike. Tanzanite couldn't afford weak mære. If one was injured, people would start believing they weren't immortal. She couldn't have that.

She tapped her diamond dagger against her palm a couple more times before thrusting it through the mære's left eye. No light sparkled through the diamond blade as it sank into the abyss. The mære barely managed a screech before it crumpled to the ground, lifeless. There was no blood. Only smoke bled from the creatures.

Such a waste.

Raising her attention above the corpse, her gaze was met with a hundred more pairs of abysmal eyes and a lone huntsman. This was all that remained of her army? Her precious army that kept the valley in line for the last century, that hunted and haunted the wicked in their footsteps by day and dreams by night, and that believed in her and served her loyally, better than even her own family.

She growled in frustration until it grew into a scream. "How many people do I have to kill to get this one job done? Kill my sisters! That is all I ask! For some measly little idiot to do this one little task! Kill them!"

She grabbed the nearest object—a bottle of mermaid stomach acid—and threw it at the huntsman's feet. He jumped back, but it splashed onto his shoes and trousers. The drops of acid ate away at the fabric. The man hurried to remove his shoes and rip away the poisoned sections of his trousers.

"Huntsman."

"Your Grace." He stopped worrying about discarding the refuse and kneeled before her. "Forgive me, I have not yet completed the task you gave me."

"I can see that. Even my mære failed to remove that stain on my happiness. They had an excuse though. They ran into an entire battalion of ogres and a dozen herds of beasts. Several of my precious mære were lost. More than I have lost in decades. Too many. What is your excuse?"

"Forgive me," he said, still bowing. "I recognized one of the men. It was my brother."

Queen Tanzanite turned sharply on her huntsman. He was supposed to be a drifter with no living family. Then again, so was she.

She scoffed. "Siblings. They are the worst." He said nothing, which was right since she hadn't asked a question. She sneered at him. "Look at you. Barefoot and ragged like the day I found you. What would you be without me?"

The young man turned away. The queen frowned deeper. That wasn't right.

"I said," she raised her voice, "what would you be without me?"

He kept his face turned away, but muttered, "Ogre food."

"Louder!"

"Ogre food!" he said, facing her, but keeping his eyes lowered. That was right.

She approached him and touched his chin until he looked up at her. "I know," she said, "how hard it can be to spill the blood of a kinsman. But they are not your family. Families support one another in their dreams. The ogres delivered you to me as a sign of their truce. Ironic, is it not? They did not know that I would make you one of my own, as I do for everyone in my kingdom. They did not know that I would support you in your dreams. Remind me, Huntsman, what is your dream?"

"Destroy the ogres."

Tanzanite smiled, but there was no mirth in her eyes. "Yes. Have I not kept my promise? Have I not seen to the death of every ogre who dared to step into Rezhina Valley? Have I not allowed you to take some of their lives with your own hands? You are safe here." For the sake of not starting another war, she'd made a treaty with the ogres. If they left her and her valley alone, she would leave them and the northern grassland kingdoms alone. Any ogres who entered the valley were disposed of by her mære.

Growing up with the war between Ormio and Huiess, she'd seen the horrors and hate it caused. The only hope of ending it was Sapphire's crazy predictions. Tanzi would unite Rezhina and make peace in the valley for a whole century. Everything she'd done— from dressing like an old hag to poisoning her foolish sisters—was to see that prophecy fulfilled.

The ogres must have finished off Uldra and the northern kingdoms, then become greedy. Or her wretched sisters had somehow made a new deal with them after waking. Why else would they send the ogress princess past the northern mountains into old Somnus? Why else would that same princess never contact her? Why else would they send an entire battalion two weeks later to rampage through old Somnus until her mære caught them?

Tanzi frowned. She had sent her mære after her sisters, not the ogres, yet they knew the order to kill any ogre that crossed their paths. Had the battalion of ogres been following or chasing her sisters?

The queen walked to her map room where a detailed map of her kingdom was sprawled across a table large enough to seat a dozen people. She sorted through the reports on ogre sightings and pillages. The first sighting in the northern-most city near the mountain pass had been of the ogress princesses four weeks ago. Then, two weeks later, a battalion had pillaged through the city. Instead of chasing the citizens westward, reports said the battalion followed the southern path of the ogress. Tanzanite had thought that was unusual when she first received the report. Several days had gone by without another incident involving her subjects. She received rumors of their passing westward, but the next sighting was her own as she watched via her mirror while her mære tore them apart.

Tanzi traced their likely path, considering the speed of their travels. They could not have stopped to plunder the abandoned cities along the coast. They had not stopped to settle. They had run…as if on a hunt.

The queen closed her eyes and reflected on the visions of her mirror from the attack. Yes, the mære had seen her sisters ride by in haste, then the ogres came into view, running—no, chasing them. Why were the ogres hunting her sisters?

She shifted through the other details of the chase. There had been a fancy stage coach with green and white shields. Uldra?

The queen's eyes snapped open. That had been more than a stage coach for interchangeable passengers. That had been a State Coach for the royal family. How had her spy network missed that passing through the mountains? No, they mentioned it passing through with the ogress princesses. Except…now her sisters drove it?

Understanding hit her like the effects of an instant poison. Her smile grew until it became a laugh. She laughed all the way back to her mirror, pausing only to ask her magic window to show her sisters to her.

"You corrupted little hypocrites," Tanzanite laughed at her sisters as if they could hear her. "You killed the ogress princess and took her carriage! You probably have the gratitude of the northern kingdoms for it, and I helped you kill off an entire battalion! Beshrews." Her laughter faltered as she realized the strength of that probability. Marin, Emer, and Pearl would have the thanks of Uldra and every northern kingdom suffering by the hands of the ogres. After gratitude came…support.

Without knowing their identities, the queen had little interest in the men traveling with her sisters. Until now. She asked her mirror to name them if it could. The mirror only had the knowledge of current events within Rezhina, but these men had spent enough time to make themselves known in Rezhina.

It named the former Princes of Braeder and Zubra and Prince Caden Seaver of Uldra. Tanzi gaped as fury and incredulity filled her. Her sisters not only managed to survive her poison, wake from Garnet's sleeping tonic, and escape their unnatural disasters surrounding them, but also to befriend the most influential men of the northern kingdoms?

"How?" Tanzanite shouted, slamming her fist against the stone wall hard enough to bleed.

Studying the interactions between her sisters and the princes, she altered her earlier thought. Her sisters had done more than simply befriended the princes. They had infected their minds with romance.

The queen snarled. "The ogres broke their side of the treaty. I suppose that means I can break my side as well. Yes, I have proved my capacity to rule these past hundred harvests. Perhaps it is time I expand my rule northward. While their princes have abandoned them, may the Uldrans praise *me* for destroying the ogres."

She began to pen a summons for soldiers. She could spare a few mære to lead the fodder, but the rest would go to the locations of the sleeping princesses. For the sake of the peace in her kingdom, she would guarantee that the others would never wake.

End of Book Three

Acknowledgements

While I've previously thanked Professor Rudy for instructing me about western European fairytales, with this book, I also want to thank my American Sign Language professors. I'll never regret those four semesters of learning about the beautiful Deaf culture. I'd also like to thank a previous project that may never see the light of day (which is ironic) because of the research into blindness that it spurred. Let this be a message to everyone; no efforts are wasted.

Speaking of influences, I'll admit, I'm not exactly grateful for the tales that inspired this book. Hans Christian Anderson liked to torture his main characters, and I personally prefer the wits of Little Red from the perspectives of Paul Delarue, James Thurber, Italo Calvino, Chiang Mi, and Roald Dahl. (Seriously, look them up. They're like girl versions of *Jack the Giant Killer*.) I really wanted to retell the story of the spunky Little Red who inspired Charles Dickens to say, "if I could have married Little Red Riding Hood, I should have known perfect bliss." Unfortunately, the story refused to come together until I switched her for the disobedient girl of Charles Perrault and Brothers Grimm. Sorry—not sorry.

If you love my cover art (I know many of you do, because you kindly say so), you can find more beautiful works by Arcane Covers.

A giant-sized thanks goes to my Alpha and Beta readers: Robyn Cheatham, Bettilee Hunt, Jim Doran, Ami, NaDell Ransom, Colleen Dowda, and Cheryl Holden. The "title" goes to Robyn and Becky Hill for helping me to finalize my title and blurbs (for this book and previous books).

As always, my biggest "thank you" goes to Michael Smith and God. I couldn't have written this book without them. While God inspires me to start, Michael keeps me going.

About the Author

C Rae D'Arc has been involved in every stage of a book's life. As a writer, editor, retailer, reader, and reviewer, she has worked four part-time jobs at once. Thankfully, one of them actually paid her. She received her Bachelors in English from Brigham Young University, where she studied ASL, British and American literature, folklore, Shakespeare, and West European fairy tales. She now lives in the Tri-Cities of Washington with her husband and Aussie dog.

PS. To save you from hiccups, D'Arc only has one syllable.

www.craedarc.com
www.facebook.com/c.rae.darc
www.instagram.com/craedarc

Fall in love with a
D'Arc Romantic Comedy

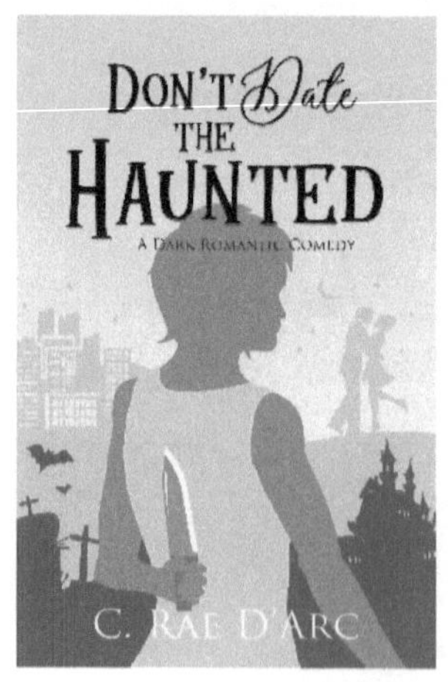